"They think we're married," Shannon said finally.

"We are, technically."

"Only because we haven't done the paperwork for a divorce."

"It's been seven years, Shannon. If you really wanted a divorce, you would have made it happen."

"I do want one, Jack." Her mouth hinted at more to come but she stayed quiet.

He hooked his thumbs in his belt loops. "For the time being, it looks like we're gonna have to play at being nice married folks until we get Dina and her baby out of this jam."

A glimmer, a flicker, a shadow rippled across her face. Her mouth thinned into a grim line.

"Pack up. We'll get a cab to the airstrip in the morning. I'll keep watch tonight. They may come back. You can tell Dina where we're headed. You have her cell number."

"And where exactly are we headed?" she said over her shoulder.

He looked into the luminous eyes of the woman who was his wife in name only, wondering what he had just gotten himself into. "Home," he said. "To Gold Bar."

Dana Mentink is a national bestselling author. She has been honored to win two Carol Awards, a HOLT Medallion and an RT Reviewers' Choice Best Book Award. She's authored more than thirty novels to date for Love Inspired Suspense and Harlequin Heartwarming. Dana loves feedback from her readers. Contact her at danamentink.com.

COWBOY BODYGUARD

DANA MENTINK

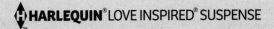

HARLEQUIN® LOVE INSPIRED® SUSPENSE

Recycling programs
for this product may
not exist in your area.

LOVE INSPIRED BOOKS

ISBN-13: 978-1-335-54387-5

Cowboy Bodyguard

Copyright © 2018 by Dana Mentink

www.Harlequin.com

Printed in U.S.A.

For by grace are ye saved through faith;
and that not of yourselves: it is the gift of God.
—Ephesians 2:8

For my darling Emily and Holly,
who inspire me every day.

ONE

Shannon Livingston ignored the splashes of blood on her scrubs. She shoved the mask off her face and dropped it into the waste container.

Her patient, T.J. Willis, was alive in Los Angeles Mercy Hospital—at least for the moment—a fall down the stairs having left him with a basilar skull fracture and internal bleeding. His rowdy biker clan was waiting for a report. Hospital security was already apprised. The nurses had done what they could to placate the members of the Scarlet Tide: easing off T.J.'s "colors" instead of cutting the clothing and making sure Willis's entourage had a private waiting area for the more than two dozen biker brothers. They'd followed hospital protocol for the known "one percenters," an ironic name to set apart the bikers who were outlaws from the 99 percent who weren't.

The bikers gathered in the waiting area were

not law-abiding motorcycle enthusiasts, according to the police bulletins. They were criminals, and they wanted only one thing from Shannon, something she could not give them: a guarantee that T.J. would be okay. She sucked in a breath and exited the recovery room and headed to the waiting area, past a nervous security guard.

The raucous conversation ended abruptly as all eyes slid to her. Shannon noticed a young woman, barely out of her teens, clutching a baby in a lace-trimmed blanket.

"I'm Cruiser. Talk to us, Doc," said the largest biker, whose face was covered by a black beard.

Cruiser was flanked by several equally hairy individuals with similar tattoos. To his right stood a tall, lanky man with his hair in a long braid, who regarded Shannon with undisguised hostility. "T.J.'s gonna live, right? He's gonna be all right?"

"I can't give you any guarantees," she said. "He sustained serious injuries in the fall."

"We know what happened," the braided man said, jutting his chin at the girl. "She did this to him, pushed him down the stairs."

"I didn't," the girl said, swallowing convulsively. "It was an accident."

Veins stood out on Cruiser's jaw. "We'll deal with her later."

Shannon's heart dropped. The woman's dark eyes caught hers, wet with tears. "What's your name?"

"Dina," she whispered. "Dina Brown."

"Not your business, Doc," Cruiser snapped. "She's ours to tend to."

Ours? As if she was some sort of property. Shannon lifted her chin. "Are you threatening her?"

He walked closer, almost close enough that his wiry beard touched her face. She did not back down, though her throat went dry. "I don't make threats," he said. "Just promises."

Shannon stood her ground until he finally backed away. She took the opportunity to swivel on her heel and make an escape, figuring this was a matter for the cops. She'd make sure they'd help Dina. On her way to place a phone call to fill them in, she was called in to assist with a cardiac emergency. It was almost an hour before she finally found her way to the break room. The door swung shut behind her, and her shoulders sagged, reminding her how long she'd been on her feet for another marathon shift. A slight figure stepped out of the shadows.

The slender brunette was clutching a bundle, tears rolling down her freckled cheeks in mascara-tinted rivulets. "Dina? What happened?"

The bundle wriggled.

"I said I had to go change Annabell, and I sneaked away. They're all over the hospital, looking for me. I hid behind a laundry cart, and I heard them. They're coming for me."

Shannon pulled a corner of the blanket aside, relieved to see a tiny pink-cheeked baby, perfect as a porcelain doll, sleeping peacefully in Dina's arms.

"She's beautiful. How old?"

The girl smiled for the first time. "Four months. She was born on Valentine's Day."

"What really happened with T.J.?"

The smile vanished. "We were arguing. I told him I was leaving. He said we belonged to him, and we'd never get away."

Shannon noted the faded bruises on the young woman's arms, the round scar on her wrist. Her pulse ticked higher as Dina continued.

"He grabbed me and started to shake me. I shoved him as hard as I could. He tripped and fell down the stairs, but he was okay. I mean, he was moving and groaning and stuff. I ran to get help, but..." The tears came faster now. "The Tide thinks I did it on purpose. I have to get out of here. I was so stupid to get involved with them."

Voices erupted in the hallway outside. Dina clung to Shannon's arm, her nails digging in.

Annabell stirred in her sleep. They had to find a quiet place where they could talk it over without running into any Tide members. Shannon grabbed her purse.

She pulled open the door and saw a man in a sport coat, a cop whom she recognized as Detective Mason. He'd interviewed her in the past about some gang-related injuries she'd treated. *He'll help.* But then she caught sight of the man across from him: Cruiser. Cruiser handed him a thick envelope. Mason put it in his coat pocket. Shannon's breath caught. Mason was on the take. How many others on the force were, too? Just as she closed the door, Cruiser glanced up and saw her. His eyes narrowed, and he took a step in her direction.

Panic roiled through her body as she shut the door and jammed a chair under the knob. She didn't know if Cruiser suspected Dina of seeking out Shannon, but he clearly wasn't thrilled to know she'd seen him with Mason. Goose bumps erupted on her arms. Whom could they trust? *Time to triage. Biggest need first. Get Dina and the baby to safety.* "There's a back way." Together, they hurried out the rear entrance, Shannon rifling through her purse. "I've got some cash. We'll get a cab."

They burst through the exit doors into a mild Los Angeles evening. It took only a moment to flag down a taxi, from the line waiting at the hospital, and hop inside. She gave him the address to a café located a few miles away. Shannon relaxed a fraction as the driver pulled from the curb, until Dina glanced at her cell-phone screen. Face gone bloodless, she turned the screen to Shannon. "It's from Cruiser."

There's nowhere to hide.

The rumble of an approaching motorcycle deafened them. "Scrunch down," she told Dina, trying not to stare out the window as the two motorcyclists drew closer, threading their way through city traffic. It was too risky to go back to her apartment. The noise and clamor of the city seemed to cage her in like prison bars.

"The police…" she whispered, too low for the cabbie to hear over his music.

Dina shook her head violently. "No. Please. The Tide has paid off some of the cops. They turn a blind eye to the drug deals for a cut of the profits." Tears rolled down her face and splashed onto the baby's cheek.

"They aren't all on the take," Shannon started. "Some of them…"

"You don't understand," she snapped. "The Tide is powerful. The cops are scared of them. If I'm found guilty of pushing T.J. down the stairs, the Tide has people in prison who will kill me. They'll take my baby. I just need to find my brother. He has connections. He'll help me."

Shannon tried to calm her hysteria. "No one is going to send you to prison for an accident. Where is your brother?"

"Central California. I don't know where exactly, but I can find him. I just need a few days. That's all. Please," she whispered. "Please."

Central California. Unexpectedly, her memory dredged up the warm springtime breezes from her hometown, Gold Bar, where she'd left behind her old life, and her first love, her husband, Jack Thorn. Though Jack traveled regularly to his uncle's farm in Santa Barbara, she'd never once reached out to see him. He was there now, according to her friend Ella's latest text, not two hours away, probably eased into a saddle in that way that made her think he was born to be on a horse. She could call him. Just for advice.

No. Too much betrayal. Too much pain. She did not have the right, even if they were still technically married. That was a mess she had yet to clean up, the legal untying of a colossal mistake.

The motorcycle pulled up alongside the cab. Cruiser scanned the street. His look was filled with hatred as his glance swept the vehicle. She thought about the girls she'd treated in her volunteer work at the women's shelter, terrified young ladies with few options and no resources. Desperate, just like Dina. The memory stiffened her spine and cemented a decision deep in her gut.

A few days, that was all. She'd escort Dina someplace safe. The cabbie made it through the light, leaving the bikers stuck behind a loaded semi. They made a move to edge onto the sidewalk, but the presence of two traffic cops was enough to dissuade them. It was the break she needed. "I've changed my mind. Take us to the nearest rental-car company," she told the cabbie.

She stared at the phone in her hand. Again, the urge to call Jack nearly overwhelmed her. Her finger hovered over the buttons.

Call him, her gut said.

Jack Thorn replayed the voice mail, again, for the dozenth time, just to be sure he wasn't losing it.

"Jack, it's Shannon. I'm in trouble. I... I don't know how to handle it. Meet me at the Park Motel, in Fairview, please, as soon as you can. I know I don't have the right to ask, but I am. I need your help. Please."

Jack stared at his phone again, trying to still the irrational thumping of his pulse as he contemplated the run-down motel from under the brim of his battered cowboy hat. Fairview was just an hour from his uncle's Santa Barbara property, where they'd been negotiating the sale of a beautiful Dutch warmblood, which would fit perfectly into the jumping sessions at his family's Gold Bar Ranch. Why had Shannon called? Why now, when he'd finally gotten things squared away in his heart, decided to make the divorce happen? Her call wasn't because of sentimental reasons—that much was clear.

I know I don't have the right to ask, but I am...

She'd gotten that part correct. She didn't have the right, even if that dusty marriage license folded in his Bible said otherwise. Just a piece of paper, which he should have shredded seven years ago. Their union was born of a time when they were both vulnerable, him missing her so badly it hurt, and her overwhelmed by the ponderous weight of the medical training that stretched before her. The marriage was a mistake. That was all. They both knew it.

So why was he here? Fairview was a nowhere town, smaller even than Gold Bar, but with none of the beauty, squashed in the shadow of a warehouse district. At least it was near a small airstrip, which was where he'd landed the Cessna. Was that why she'd chosen the meeting place? Questions tumbled in his mind, along with the worry that she had not responded to any of his follow-up texts, just like she'd avoided his calls and declined to talk about the state of their farcical marriage in her first few months of medical school. He was a file she'd put away in the drawer and refused to open. She was a song that played endlessly in his ears and simply would not fade away. He'd finally driven to her medschool campus midway through her first year and waited four hours to speak with her.

"We can't keep going like this. I know you want a divorce. We should end things, then. Legally."

"I just can't get into it, Jack. Not now."

"When, then?"

Not ever, it seemed to him. So they lived in a legal limbo: married, but not. He hadn't seen her in over a year, their last encounter being an accidental meeting when she'd come to Gold Bar to visit her mother. It was a hot-cheeked, goosefleshed, endless few minutes. She'd been talking to a man at the inn, and a flash of something had seared through him. It didn't take any skin off his nose to live with a secret marriage, but what about when she met someone else?

His palms were sweaty as he approached Room Seven. He'd faced down wild horses, fires and floods, and recently a murderer bent on killing his twin brother Owen's now fiancée, Ella, but he'd never had to battle his nerves so hard to get them to obey. He forced his legs into motion, wiped his clammy palms on his jeans, straightened his Stetson and rapped softly on the warped wood. The door opened, and there she stood, Shannon Livingston. *Shannon Livingston Thorn*, his mind amended cruelly. Her long dark hair, the heavy curtain he'd trailed his fingers through so many times, was loose and tangled, her eyes the same flecked gold of new-spun honey, but now they did not hold that gleam of cockiness, only fear.

And there he was, a six-foot tall, gangly limbed cowboy, struck completely dumb.

While he stood mute as stone, she took his hand, her fingers cold on his skin, and pulled him inside the minuscule room. As he automatically removed his hat, his mouth dropped open at the sight of a young woman, who was sitting on one of the twin beds, rocking a baby, of all things.

He swiveled his gaze back to Shannon. "Let's hear it."

She huffed out a breath, pacing the mud-colored carpet. Her words came out in a rush. "Jack, this is Dina Brown and her daughter, Annabell. She's in trouble. I need to hide them for a few days. We've been driving in a rental car, and the men who are after her somehow caught up with us again. I lost them, I think, but I got scared and called you. I would have called home, to Gold Bar, but…"

Hide them? What happened? His eyes wandered over the faded bruises on the young woman's arms, a shiny cigarette burn near the wrist. A stream of other questions coursed through his mind, along with the most important one. *Why did you call* me? Instead, he settled on, "Who and why?"

She held up a palm, once more the in-control, unflappable Shannon. "Let me help Dina get a bottle ready for the baby, and then I'll tell you everything. Promise."

To give himself time to process, he looked around. A grocery bag with a loaf of bread sticking out the top, a paper map, keys to a rental car. On the run, instead of calling the police? Scared enough that she would take on the protection of a young woman and her baby? Maybe it wasn't so hard to believe. Shannon was the most fearless person he knew, except for his younger brother Keegan, and she would face down anyone to right a wrong…unless she was the one who had inflicted it. He smothered the flicker of anger.

Shannon shook up a baby bottle and handed it to Dina. "I know this is crazy, Jack, but I need to get her somewhere safe until she finds her brother. There's a gang after her, the Scarlet Tide. You know of them?"

"Can't live in this state and not know of them. The cops…"

"We can't trust them, not now. They…"

Her eyes rounded as a rumble filled the air, so loud it became a roar that shook the walls. He strode to the window and pulled the curtain aside a few inches. Two motorcycles, Harley-Davidsons, similar to the one Keegan rode in his wilder days, idled in the parking lot. The guys were big, one bearded, the other sporting a bandanna around his head, a braid poking out from underneath it.

"Cruiser," Dina said, mouth trembling, as she peeked past his shoulder, while the baby sucked contentedly. "And Viper." The bottle shook in her hand. "They found us again, and now they're gonna kill me and take my baby." The last bit came out as a whimper.

Shannon pulled Dina away from the window and folded her and the baby into an embrace. The gesture made his breath catch, for some reason. Both women looked at him.

"Hide in the bathroom," Jack commanded. Dina ran with the baby, almost closing the door behind her except for a crack.

Shannon's eyes were unreadable, shimmering with tension and something else. Guilt, probably, though she wouldn't let that trouble her for more than a moment. She must have been desperate indeed to call him up.

As Jack continued to peer out, the two bikers surveyed the row of hotel rooms, considering. They weren't sure which one was Shannon's. They would wait, take shifts, and eventually, they'd know. There was no time to get the women out a rear exit without being detected, unless they climbed out the high bathroom window, and that would be tricky with a baby. They were trapped.

He could tell by Shannon's quickened breaths that she'd come to the same conclusion. Her look to him was one of barely contained panic. His brain said call the cops. His gut said there was no other way, but somehow, his heart overruled them both.

He turned around and handed Shannon his cell. "Tell Dina to lock the bathroom door and call the police."

"But…"

"Do it, Shannon."

"Dina," Shannon called. She pushed her way in. Her gasp told him the truth before she emerged with the baby in her arms.

"She bolted. Climbed out the window and left the baby on a towel. The diaper bag is stashed under the sink." Shannon fingered a piece of paper scribbled with a lipstick note. "'I'll be back in two days. Keep her safe for me. Don't let them take her.'"

He met Shannon's eyes, the iridescent pools that pulled him in. "How do you want to play this?"

"I promised to buy Dina a few days to find her brother. If we call the cops now…"

He nodded. "Baby goes into foster care, most likely."

Shannon bit her lip. "If the gang takes the baby, Dina will never get her back…" She shook her head. "I promised. A few days, I promised."

"A promise is a promise," he said, trying not to choke on the irony.

She lifted her chin, voice gone hard. "I understand if you don't want any part of this. It's not your mess. I shouldn't have called you."

He didn't answer. Then he clapped on his Stetson, threw open the door and strode out, Shannon on his heels, still clutching the baby. That hadn't changed, anyway. Shannon had never shied away from trouble.

The riders approached quickly, coming up close, too close. Viper spoke first. "It's her. The doctor."

"What are you doing here, Doc? Saw you beelining from the hospital," Cruiser said. "Sudden vacation?"

Jack straightened to his full height, a good

four inches taller than either man. "Who wants to know?"

Cruiser cocked his head. "Who are you, Cowboy?"

"Name's Jack Thorn. Yours?"

"Not here for a meet and greet."

Jack stared him down. "Then why are you here?"

"I want the girl and the baby."

Jack arched an eyebrow. "I don't have a girl and a baby to hand over—not that I would anyway."

"So, who do you think you are? John Wayne?" Cruiser glared.

Jack didn't answer, just stared.

Viper spoke up. "Doc treated our brother T.J. back at the hospital. We think she's hiding somebody who pushed him down the stairs. Girl Doc here is a liar."

"First point, she's not a girl," Jack said, looping an arm around Shannon's waist. She went rigid. Every cell in his body felt stunned by the physical connection, as if some deep part of him remembered the woman he ached to forget. He punched the feelings back. "This is a woman, a doctor, and she's here with me, nobody else, so watch your mouth."

Cruiser's hands bunched into fists. Jack kept his palm relaxed on her hip, ready. Anticipating an animal's reaction was nothing new for him. He could tell when a horse was about to bolt, to kick, to struggle. Cruiser was going to make a move and soon.

Cruiser's brow furrowed. "I think you're lying, too."

"I don't care what you think."

"Who are you, Cowboy?"

His mind whirled, searching and discarding ideas.

If things got physical, it would probably end with the baby being taken and Shannon hurt. Best to talk his way out of it.

"Like I said, name's Jack." He held his chin high. "I'm her husband."

Husband. The word seemed to flutter in the wind like a Fourth of July flag. Viper strode past them and pushed into the hotel room. After a moment, he returned. "No one else there."

Cruiser's eyes narrowed. "And I suppose that's your baby?"

You said it. I didn't.

TWO

Jack felt Shannon pull away a fraction, heard a soft exhalation of air.

When Cruiser took a step toward the door, Shannon moved to meet him. "Stay away from my baby."

Cruiser smiled. "Going all Mama Bear on me now? Baby's pretty young to be traveling." He jutted his chin. "Bringing it to a hotel in the middle of the sticks?"

Jack shrugged. "It was a good halfway point. We're meeting up for a much-needed vacation," he continued. "Our jobs keep us too busy, don't they, Shan?" He nuzzled her ear, dizzied by the feel of her warm skin, his brain wondering what in the world he was playing at.

"Uh-huh," she mumbled, heat rising off her.

"I think you're lying," Cruiser said. "If you're married, where's the ring?"

Jack smiled. "I thought we'd already covered that I don't care what you think. Cowboys and doctors have to use their hands a lot. Rings are inconvenient when you're saddling horses, not that it's your business."

Cruiser glared at him. "I still think you're lying, Cowboy, and if I find out you're hiding Dina, I'm gonna kill you both and take what's ours—Dina and her baby."

Jack released Shannon and stepped forward, every muscle taut. He came nose to nose with Cruiser. "No one," he murmured, "is going to touch my wife."

Cruiser raised a fist, and Jack did the same, jerking his head toward the building.

"All right, but before we get this rodeo started, here's a tip. Make sure the camera gets your good side," Jack said.

Cruiser jerked, gaze finding the security camera mounted on the wall. He stepped back a pace, breathing hard. "I want Dina and the baby. They belong to the Tide. Anyone who gets in my way is my enemy. The Tide doesn't forget, and we don't forgive. We are going to be watching you." He stalked back to his bike, along with the other man, and drove off in a roar of exhaust. Jack led Shannon back into the hotel room.

Seconds ticked in awkward silence between them. How could he explain what he'd done letting them think the baby was theirs and he and

Shannon a loving couple? He could come up with nothing, so he stayed quiet.

"They think we're married," she said finally.

"We are, technically."

"Only because we haven't done the paperwork for a divorce."

"It's been seven years, Shannon. If you really wanted a divorce, you would have made it happen."

"I do want one, Jack." Her mouth hinted at more to come, but she stayed quiet. He wanted to kiss her then, to press her lips to his and find out the truth. Mouths lied, but kisses didn't.

He hooked his thumbs in his belt loops. "For the time being, it looks like we're gonna have to play at being nice married folks until we get Dina and her baby out of this jam."

A glimmer, a flicker, a shadow, rippled across her face. Her mouth thinned into a grim line.

"Anyway," Jack said, putting them back on safe ground, "it bought us some time so Dina can find her brother."

"I'm not sure anymore…" She pressed a trembling hand to her mouth.

"I am. Pack up. We'll get a cab to the airstrip in the morning. I'll keep watch tonight. They may come back. Not that easily put off. You can tell Dina where we're headed. You have her cell number."

"And where exactly are we headed?" she said over her shoulder.

He looked into the luminous eyes of the woman who was still his wife—legally, anyway—wondering what he had just gotten himself into. "Home," he said. "To Gold Bar."

Emotions tumbled through Shannon's insides as Jack landed the plane on the neglected airstrip on her uncle Oscar's property. The sky was mellowing into a palette of lustrous sunset golds, set off by the brilliant green hills. After seven years, with as many visits as she could manage, Gold Bar was just as gorgeous as she remembered, and just as claustrophobic. It was a small town, where everybody knew everything, a place she would probably never return to if her mother and uncle were not still residents.

The pastures of Jack's family's Gold Bar Ranch were dotted with contented horses that meandered, tails swishing, over the thousand acres. She thought of Jack's brothers. A new structure was visible, set apart from the main house. Jack's brother Barrett and his new wife, Shelby, lived there. Jack's twin, Owen, was engaged to Shannon's best friend, Ella Cahill, a farrier who had narrowly escaped being framed for the murder of a local heiress's nephew by a merciless con man. It pained her that she hadn't even known about Ella's dire situation until after it was resolved. Too busy to take calls, she'd told herself. *Too busy to be a friend.*

She eyed Jack. He had the same angular features and strong jaw, but there was something more pinched about his mouth, and his denim-blue eyes were harder. He wore his favorite cowboy boots, the ones he'd steadfastly refused to replace, instead having them resoled again and again. The fragrance of his barn jacket teased her, holding the faintest scent of a life far away, oiled leather, hay, the ranch. His life, not hers. *You should ask about his brothers, make small talk.* But the memory of a long-ago conversation with Jack robbed her of the words. Seven years ago, practically before the ink was dry on their marriage certificate, she'd told him their impulsive marriage was over.

It was a mistake, Jack.

As if she was critiquing a medical chart, instead of dooming a marriage.

I was scared, confused. I'm leaving for med school, and that's all I can focus on.

I'm patient, he'd said.

I'm not coming back to Gold Bar, Jack. Not as your wife.

The marriage was an error in judgment. She'd been overwhelmed, and Jack had refused to admit that they'd outgrown each other. *You did what you had to do.* Now, if she could just get through this without losing everything she'd worked for. In typical Jack fashion, he had not pressed her for details about her current situation, allowing her to share as much as she knew. Jack was patient; he was completely her opposite.

The facts seemed clear enough. Dina was being abused by a man who lay in a coma for which the Scarlet Tide blamed her. The Los Angeles detective who had been investigating the case was on the take, and thanks to Jack, they could keep Annabell safe until Dina returned. John Larraby, an officer with the Gold Bar Police, was a high-school peer of theirs, and though she'd never liked him personally, maybe he could be trusted to help. It would be so much easier to tell him everything, but what would happen to Annabell? Whatever Dina had or hadn't done, she did not deserve to lose her baby.

Shannon checked her phone messages. Her supervising physician was unhappy at her sudden departure, which she'd blamed on an emergency. It was the truth. What bigger emergency was there than a bunch of bikers ready to abduct a scared teen mom and her baby?

She'd had no choice but to run, but the potential professional consequences were terrifying. She'd labored for years to reach the final stages of her emergency-room internship. What if she lost it all? Then what would she be? Who would she be? She realized Jack was staring at her.

"Did you tell anyone we were coming to Gold Bar?" he asked, eyes flicking from his cell-phone screen to her.

"Only Dina. I texted her, like you said."

"Work?"

"I phoned to tell them I had to take an emergency leave, but I didn't mention where I was headed."

He frowned, blue eyes darkening to the color of a restless sea.

"Why?"

"Because my brother just texted me that Larraby's at the house, asking for you."

Cold prickles erupted all over her skin. Had Mason alerted the local police somehow? But how would he know where they'd gone?

Her mind followed the trail. He might have found out from the hospital about her hastily arranged vacation, used his police connections to discover her hometown, checked flight plans and contacted local police. In other words, he'd made a guess that had paid off.

"We can't trust the cops," she said, holding the baby, as Jack helped her out of the plane and into a dusty SUV. "Detective Mason is in the Tide's pocket. Larraby will believe what he says."

"We may not have a choice."

As they drove to the ranch, Shannon frantically tried to figure out what she would say to Larraby, or the Thorns, for that matter.

She knew her own cheeks were flushed red as they entered the Thorn home. Jack's parents, Tom and Evie, had been kind and gracious to her, but she had not seen them since she left for med school.

"I'm not going to tell anyone about this," Jack had said after their city-hall marriage in Southern California. *"I want to tell my family properly, to present you as my bride."*

But that time had never arrived, and Jack had revealed during the flight that he'd never gotten around to telling them at all. So how were they going to explain it? It was ludicrous.

Her feet dragged like anchors as they neared the front door. The baby began to cry.

Evie Thorn's eyes opened wide in shock as she looked from Shannon to the bundle in her arms. "Shannon… I… A…baby? I didn't know."

Me neither. Shannon gulped, with no idea what to say, but Evie offered a shaky hug, brushed back her bob of graying hair and ushered them in. John Larraby stood at the table with Evie's husband, Tom, and youngest son, Keegan, who flashed her a puzzled smile, a half-eaten apple between his fingers. Owen and Ella were away for a while, Tom explained, visiting friends and purchasing a new wheelchair for Ella's sister, Betsy.

Larraby greeted them. If he was surprised at her sudden arrival with a baby in tow, he did not show it. "I got a call from Detective Hal Mason in Los Angeles."

So it had been Mason who called. She rocked the baby, who had begun to fuss.

"What did he say?" Jack asked.

Larraby's dark gaze settled on her. "Says he wants to talk to Shannon Livingston about a patient she treated recently." He raised an eyebrow. "And to congratulate you both on the new baby."

The baby wriggled against Shannon, as if she could feel the embarrassment rising off her in waves. "I...uh..."

The announcement took the Thorn family by storm. Evie's mouth was open in a wide O-shape of surprise. Keegan, too, was slack-jawed with astonishment. Only Tom seemed cool and collected.

"So, he told you about the baby?" Jack shot her a look, and in a flash of cold fear, she understood. The only way Mason could have known that Shannon was caring for Annabell was if the two gang members had told him. So, it was true. Mason was on the take.

"Well, this is a surprise, of course. We didn't know that you two were still together," Tom said.

"Should I pass along your cell-phone number to Mason?" Larraby asked.

Jack didn't answer, but he locked eyes on Shannon's. She knew him well enough to know the nonverbal. *Your call.* Should she lie to Larraby or trust him?

She wanted to straighten out the whole ridiculous scenario. *I'm not going to fold neatly into this family and start raising children in Gold Bar. It's all a ruse, a misunderstanding that we're going to clear up right now.*

Shannon took a breath and made a decision. "She's not ours. She's a friend's, but there are good reasons why we're pretending otherwise."

Larraby hooked his thumbs in his gun belt. "Might this friend be the person the Tide believes pushed their brother T.J. down the stairs?"

Seconds ticked by that felt like hours. "This friend," Shannon said carefully, "is a nineteen-year-old who has been beaten and terrorized by her boyfriend. She's been in and out of shelters, afraid to stay and unable to leave for fear of what the Tide will do. She's done nothing wrong. We are pretending to be this baby's parents to give her a few days to find her brother. It's her only chance to get herself and her baby out."

He was quiet for a moment. "Motorcycle gang

members are tough to prosecute. They stick together no matter what. They'd take a bullet for each other."

"So would we," Keegan said.

Larraby's mouth tightened. "I'm going to lay it out for you. I don't like Mason. We worked together on a task force because the Aces are the local motorcycle gang in this region, and they are sworn enemies of the Tide. We had some trouble a while back when the Tide came to town seeking revenge for some slight or another." His gaze drifted momentarily to Keegan, who stared right back. "You know all about the Aces, don't you, Keegan?"

"I was only a prospect," Keegan said. "I never patched in."

Larraby's mouth quirked. "Too bad. You would have fit right in."

"I won't have that talk in this house," Tom said. "Past is past."

Shannon knew of the rage that simmered between the biological half brothers. Keegan was the product of an affair between Bryce Larraby and Keegan's mother. Bryce had never acknowledged Keegan, and the hurt ran deep. Keegan's troubled youth had led him into all sorts of difficulties, until the Thorn family took him in and eventually adopted him.

"Let him talk," Keegan said, eyes sparking. "Makes him feel like a big man, like dear old dad."

Tom put a hand on his youngest son's shoulder, the pressure quieting him.

Larraby shrugged. "Personally, I think Mason is on the take, always has been, but no one can make anything against him stick. I don't believe a word he says."

Jack stared at Larraby. "So where does that leave us?"

"You're protecting Dina Brown's baby," Larraby went on, "and as far as I'm concerned, that's your business. I've got bigger problems right now, because the Aces are prepping for their national run, heading for a convention in Reno. They'll be in the vicinity, and if the Tide shows up looking for the baby, there's gonna be a turf war." His gaze drifted momentarily to Keegan, who stared right back.

Larraby's radio squawked, and he silenced it, turning to Jack and Shannon. "If you're hiding this baby from the Tide, you better hide her well. That includes keeping your secrets from Mason. Do you understand what I'm saying to you?"

Jack nodded. Shannon didn't answer.

Larraby waited a beat. "I will back up your story to Mason for a few days. As far as I know, you two are married and have a new little bundle of joy. If I get any orders to start an official investigation, though, then no more hands off. Understood?"

"Yes," Jack said. "You're giving us time. Thank you."

"Don't thank me." Larraby strode to the door. "The Tide is as dangerous as they come, almost as dangerous as a crooked cop. They want Dina, and they will go after the baby to find her. Watch your backs."

The door closed behind him.

Evie stood, hands on hips. "All right, Jack William Thorn. I know you're the strong, silent type, but now you're going to spill it."

Shannon knew what her unspoken thoughts were. *Why would you take all this risk with a woman who abandoned you, a woman who wants nothing to do with Gold Bar?*

Jack blew out a breath. "It's complicated, Mama."

She snorted. "Not really. What's going on between you two?"

Keegan turned a chair around and straddled it, a mischievous smile on his face. "I can't wait to hear this."

Shannon watched Jack heave in a breath and drop the bomb. "Shannon and I are married," he said. "We have been for seven years now."

THREE

It took Jack a while to go through the whole story again. Parts of it, he could hardly wrap his mind around himself. He was a husband to Shannon, sort of, and caring for an actual, real live infant.

"So, you've been married?" Keegan said. "All this time? And you kept it a secret?"

He looked away from the merriment in Keegan's eyes and the hurt in his mother's, feeling lower than pond scum.

Shannon cleared her throat. "We… I…realized the marriage was a mistake right after we went through with it. We're getting a divorce, but we just haven't gotten around to it."

Evie straightened and stared at Shannon. "This is too much. Keeping this secret was hurtful enough, but now finding out you've been stringing him along for seven years?"

Shannon went hot all over.

"Mama," Jack said. "This is as much my fault

as hers. I'm sorry I didn't tell you earlier. I just...
didn't want to talk about it."

"You don't want to talk about anything,"
Keegan said. "Except horses and saddles. Silent as a man being shaved, as Granddad used
to say." He was still enjoying the whole drama.

The baby's fussing turned into an all-out holler.

"I'm going to find Annabell some baby things."
Evie walked by, and Tom caught her around the
waist.

"I'll help." He looked at her and squeezed
again. Their eyes met, and she sighed, some of
the anger leaking out of her. She did not exactly
smile at Shannon, but her tone was softer.

"We'll do everything we can to help you
both."

"Thank you," Shannon said.

The time was broken up by his mother's forays
into the attic to find clothes, mostly in blues and
yellows, leftovers from their babyhoods.

"The Thorn boys were all big tykes," she said,
"so little Annabell will be swimming in them,
but at least she'll have clean clothes to wear.
Look, though. I found some pink things. Must
have been from when I was expecting Barrett. I
thought for sure he was going to be a girl."

Keegan laughed. "He would have been one un-
attractive girl. Big as an ox and just as graceful."

Shannon mumbled a thank-you.

Jack marveled at the sheer joy on his mother's face as she sorted the clothes to take them to the wash. Even though the baby was not her kin, and they'd just shocked her badly, she had instantly offered up whatever she had. He blinked back a strong surge of emotion. His mother had a true servant's heart. She didn't deserve the hurt he'd dished out, not one bit of it.

She even managed to locate a bassinet, which made her eyes swim. Barrett ambled into the room with his arm around his wife, Shelby. Jack knew Keegan had filled him in on the latest bombshell.

"Perfect timing," his mother said. "Barrett, can you go pick up diapers? I'm thinking a newborn size? She's four months old, but tiny."

Jack's oldest brother rubbed his beard and broke out in a look of sheer panic when his mother began to expound over the various diaper options.

"Uh... I thought they just came in a one-size-fits-all kinda deal."

Shelby laughed. "I'll go with him. We'll get bottles and formula and all the trimmings. Good practice for the future," she said, elbowing him.

The expression of half terror, half longing on Barrett's face made them all laugh.

When they finally finished rich bowls of stew

with crusty slabs of bread, Shannon and Keegan tackled the dishes, while Evie rocked the baby in the adjoining room. Jack sank into a chair next to her. "I'm sorry."

"You should be," she said with spirit. "I always told you keeping a secret is the same as lying, and here you were keeping quiet about a thing as important as marriage. Inexcusable."

"Yes, ma'am."

She skimmed the baby's downy head with her cheek. "Is it what you wanted, Jackie? The separation and the divorce?"

Her hands were so strong, he thought, calloused and capable, but she held the baby so tenderly. "I wanted her, Mama. I wanted Shannon."

"Still?"

He shook his head. "I only need to be kicked in the teeth once to learn my lesson." Part of his heart would always want her, but wanting and trusting were two different breeds.

"So, it's going to be a divorce, then? When the baby is safe?"

Divorce. Ugly word. He swallowed, throat dust-dry. "Yeah."

She bit her lip. "But this is probably painful for you. I mean, pretending to live as Shannon's husband…"

It had taken him seven years to excise her from his every thought, but he was stronger now, over it, over her. Their marriage was made of flimsy paper. They were joined by nothing more concrete than words on a certificate. "We have to continue on, just until Dina makes contact with her brother. Then, after that…" He shrugged. "Nothing has changed."

"Nothing?" She looked deep into his eyes.

He nodded. *Nothing.*

"Are you sure it isn't better to give Annabell to the police, in spite of what Larraby said?"

"No, not sure, but I saw the bruises on Dina's arms, Mama, the burns." His fingers gripped the chair arm, fighting down the anger he felt that a man would choose to dominate a woman, physically hurt the mother of his own child. "We have to give her a chance to get free of the Tide."

"But, Jackie." Her voice was a soft murmur. "Shannon?"

Shannon looked over her shoulder at that moment. He glanced back, telling her silently and reminding himself. *There's nothing between us, Shannon. Don't worry. I know that.*

She turned away, wave of dark hair falling across the curve of her cheek, hiding herself from him, like she did from the rest of the world. Hurt thrummed again through his chest.

They decided it would be best to dive into the next round of explanations with Shannon's mother the following morning, since Shannon could hardly keep her eyes open. The baby's bassinet was next to the guest-room bed, where Shannon would sleep.

Though his body was wrung out with fatigue, he found himself still dressed, pacing his tiny room, filled with energy that no amount of reading or sit-ups could dissipate. He longed to play his guitar. Instead, he rummaged through his drawer until he found the small box that he had not been able to open since she'd returned it to him. The diamond set in the gold engagement band glimmered at him, taunting him for his stupidity. Six months of savings and weeks agonizing over the style, it had meant everything, and now it was only a dust catcher. Maybe that was what it had always been. He shoved it back in the drawer, pulled on his boots and let himself out.

The ranch at night always soothed him. There was music in the hush of the breeze stirring the grass and the springtime frog symphony echoing in the creek bed. Quiet places spoke to his soul—always had. Sunset brought the end to the clamor of horse trailers coming and going on their thousand-acre property, where they boarded and trained some sixty horses at a time. Nighttime held no clang of Ella's hammer on the anvil as she crafted new horseshoes, no buzz of Keegan's motorcycle along Oscar's unused airstrip that Jack was saving every penny to buy.

The only thing better than the quiet of the sleeping ranch was the divine peace he got when he flew his Cessna.

Lady, his mare, was sidled up to the split-rail fence, and Jack was surprised to see Shannon there, a blanket clutched around her, stroking Lady's neck with tentative fingers. He cleared his throat so as not to startle her.

She jumped, shooting a guilty look at him. "The baby is sleeping."

"They do that from time to time, I hear."

Shannon's long fingers made trails in Lady's coat.

"You always wanted me to learn to ride."

Pushed her to, as a matter of fact. Softly insistent, as was his way. The quietest bull in the china shop. "Shouldn't have pressed."

"Well, what self-respecting resident of Gold Bar doesn't know how to ride a horse, right?" Her tone was bitter, brows drawn when she turned to him. "I never fit in here, no matter how much you wanted me to."

"You could have, if you slowed down for a hot minute and gave it a chance."

He expected anger. The tremble of her lip surprised him. "I can't slow down, Jack. Not ever. I wish I could, but unless I'm in high gear, I feel like a failure." She rested her forehead on the fence, and the surrender in it broke his heart.

He moved closer, reaching out toward her slender shoulders, the craving strong. Something told him his touch would not be welcome. Not anymore. He froze, and she straightened and strode back into the house, posture hunched.

Stroking Lady's neck, he watched Shannon go, sorrow knifing him swiftly and mercilessly for all the ways they'd failed each other.

Shannon dreaded explaining the whole bizarre situation to her mother, but it had to be better than staying with the Thorns, who were polite, in spite of everything. She phoned the hospital to learn that T.J. was still in a coma. The Tide remained at his bedside, minus Cruiser, according to the night nurse. Since Evie was still laundering baby clothes, and Jack had a trailer full of newly arrived horses to unload, it was not until the afternoon that they left for the Gold Nugget Inn. By that time, Shannon was about ready to commandeer the keys and drive herself.

Her mother, Hazel, swathed in a checkered apron, met them in the lovely front parlor of the Gold Nugget Inn, which was mercifully empty of guests. She limped up on her cane, and Shannon felt a stab of guilt that she had not been able to visit more. Each visit left her riddled with guilt at leaving her mother, who'd lost her leg to diabetes. But Hazel would not tolerate the merest suggestion that Shannon should take any time off to tend to her, nor hire extra help at the Inn.

"You gotta fly, honey," she'd said. *"You were born to do it."*

Now tears coursed down Hazel's plump cheeks, and her uncle, Oscar, kept scratching his white beard in puzzlement as the three followed Hazel and Oscar to the empty dining room and closed the glass-paned doors.

"You're married?" Hazel wiped her eyes.

Shannon heard Jack let out a breath. "Technically, yes, but nothing has changed. We just haven't gotten a divorce yet. We're pretending we're Annabell's parents to protect Dina, until she can find her brother. Officer Larraby knows the truth, and the Thorns. We need you to keep the secret. There are very bad people looking for the baby."

Her mother shook her head. "I always dreamed about you getting married, Shannon, but this…" She shrugged, and Shannon realized how much their hasty action, and the concealment of it, had cost their families.

I'll get married someday, she wanted to say. *When I meet the right person.* But the words felt wrong in her mouth.

"We'll do whatever you need, of course. I'm so happy to have you here." Her eyes riveted on Annabell. "May I hold her?"

Shannon handed the infant to her mother, who wore an expression of such rapture, it made Shannon squirm.

"Is it okay if we stay here? Just for a few days?"

"Of course it is," her mother said, eyes glued to the baby's every movement. "We'll put you in the Garden Room. No one is in the Night's Stay Room, either, so you can use that if you need extra space for the baby's things."

Shannon had always loved the Night's Stay Room, which adjoined the larger Garden Room. In the 1850s, customers would sometimes pay for their lodging with a pouch full of gold dust, and Hazel had discovered, in the old attic, a genuine brass scale, complete with weights. How many times had Shannon sneaked into that room when it wasn't rented out, fascinated by the mechanism that analyzed so precisely, neatly measured value? She loved the precision of it—no ambiguity, unlike every other part of life.

Oscar fidgeted. "Sure, sure. That'll do. Slow season before summer arrives. We got a room for you, Shannon, but, uh, well…"

Shannon frowned. "What is it, Uncle Oscar? You've never been any good at beating around the bush."

"Uh, I get it that you're trying to convince folks you're married and raising a baby and all, but it doesn't seem proper…"

Shannon finally got it, and a flood of heat went to her cheeks. Jack wore a pained expression.

"He can bunk with me," Oscar said. "It's right across from yours, on the top floor."

"It's not necessary…" she started, but how exactly were they supposed to carry on the happy family facade with her staying at the inn and him at the Gold Bar? She swallowed. "It's only for a little while, until we locate Dina's brother."

"Sure, sure," Oscar said.

"I'll rock the baby for a while, shall I?" her mother said.

Just don't get used to it, Mom, she wanted to say. *I'm not back together with Jack, and there are no babies in our future.* But it tugged at her heart to consider how much she'd disappointed the woman who'd been her only true champion. *I'll do better, Mom.*

A frown crossed her mother's face. "Honey, I just remembered something. I got a phone call yesterday afternoon. Someone who said they were your friend and they'd heard you were home for a visit. They wanted to chat with you."

Her stomach dropped. "Who?"

"They didn't give a name. Someone with a real raspy voice."

"What did you tell them?"

"I… I told them you were coming soon. I'm sorry." She frowned. "Was that bad?"

"It's okay. You didn't know. Did he or she leave a number?"

"No, and the ancient rotary phone we have here doesn't show recent callers or anything fancy like that. All I can tell you is it was a local call."

"Local?" Jack frowned.

She nodded. "I have to press a button to accept if it's a long-distance call. Like I said, ancient technology."

"Mason's still in Los Angeles," Shannon said. "As far as I know, and it couldn't be Cruiser."

"Could we have a third party involved here?" Jack said.

Shannon blew out a breath. "Why not? Seems like everyone in the world is after us."

"We'll sort it out, Shan."

She shouldered her bag, desperate to get upstairs and away from Jack's quiet gaze. Turmoil bubbled in her stomach. Jack stopped her near the spiral staircase. He moved close, standing a full head taller than her, shoulders broad and strong. He was lithe as a cat in spite of his bulk, a trait she'd always admired.

"Here," he said without preamble, holding something out to her.

The slender circle of gold fell into her palm,

sending ripples of pain through every nerve as she recognized it. Her wedding ring.

"Jack, this isn't…"

"I know what it is and isn't," he said sharply. "You're playing a part, and so am I." His eyes shone stark blue, like the interior part of the flame that burns the hottest. "Take it."

Unable to answer, she shoved the ring on her finger, turned on her heel and marched up the steps without looking back.

Shannon jolted awake. Moonlight streamed through the crack in the curtains. The clock read 3:15 a.m. She sat up. The baby was asleep, breathing regularly in the bassinet next to her. She was swaddled in the pink pajamas Evie had found in the attic. Nothing in the room explained what had disturbed Shannon's fitful rest.

She padded to the window and looked out over the lush hillside that bordered the main road. As she raised her hand to move the curtain farther aside, the moonlight captured the gold on her left ring finger.

You're playing a part, and so am I. The bitterness in his voice cut deep. She pulled on a robe and tiptoed downstairs for a glass of water. Built when Gold Bar was a bustling mining town, the inn was never silent. There was a constant melody of creaking floorboards, gurgling pipes and the hooting of the screech owl that lived in the tallest pine. How different from the rush of city noise. Lost in thought, she stepped into the kitchen. As she opened the cupboard for a glass, a calloused palm wrapped around her mouth from behind, smothering her scream. Whiskers tickled her ear, sour breath hot on her cheek.

"Well, hello, Doc," Cruiser murmured. "Enjoying your vacation?"

She gasped, and he eased his hand away a fraction. "How did you know I was here?"

"A little birdie told me. Drove right up from SoCal, soon as I knew where you were."

A little birdie. The anonymous person who'd called the inn. Shannon wriggled and thrashed, but he held on, his arms like bands of steel. "Stay quiet," he said. "You don't want to wake up your mother, right? Or the baby? Heard it was a girl. Ain't that a coincidence? Dina had herself a girl also, 'bout the same size as yours, I figure. What do you know about that?"

Slowly he turned her around, arm pressed across her windpipe, pinning her against the cupboard. Her hands clawed his forearm. His eyes narrowed. "Got a wedding ring now, too?"

"I told you," she gasped. "The baby is mine— mine and Jack's."

"I think you're lying, and there's a penalty for lying. Want to know what it is?"

Now she was fighting for breath, and she knew she did not have long before she blacked out. If that happened, Annabell would be easy prey, and if Oscar, Hazel or Jack got in Cruiser's way…

"I'm not lying," she said.

He pressed harder, and her vision began to blur. "Nighty night, Doc."

FOUR

The music floated through Jack's earbuds, drowning out the sound of Oscar's snores and making Jack long for his guitar. He'd often thought he should have picked up another instrument to avoid the guitar-strumming cowboy stereotype, but he'd never cared much what anyone else thought of him anyway. His fingers itched for the strings the way they had since he was four years old. Jack could never be coerced, bribed or cajoled into playing for family gatherings. Music was a private pleasure, one he'd finally shared with Shannon when they'd dated for six months, after she'd arrived the summer of his junior year of high school.

"Please, Jack. Just one song. Something that will make me cry." She'd beg him to play for her as they sat on their favorite hilltop overlooking the valley. And he would play anything she wanted, anything that would move her and feed her soul. He'd played her favorite piece, "Mal-

lorca," the day her father left abruptly, the beginning and the end of everything, it seemed to Jack. She'd refused to tell him anything, and that was the day she'd started holding back, shutting down her feelings in a sealed vault he could not breach. He should have realized that something had changed in her, and so had the future they'd imagined together. The lovely piece thrummed through him now, memories of their youth entwined with the melody. He found himself playing it sometimes late at night, despising himself for his weakness.

Some tough cowboy, strumming sad songs at night and pining for lost love. Ridiculous.

Something intruded on his reverie. Still clothed in his jeans and a T-shirt, since he hadn't packed a bag, he felt the slight vibration that made the photo above his bed rattle. Pulling out the earbuds, he sat up and listened. He heard nothing, but his gut was still tight. His twin brother, Owen, often said instinct was the quietest voice that shouted the loudest. For some reason, his instincts were hollering now.

He tiptoed out of bed and shuffled down the hallway, barefoot. All the doors were closed, and there was no sound of movement. Should he knock at Shannon's door? Risk scaring her and waking the baby? Or should he send a text, which might startle her as badly as a knock? She was a light sleeper. She had to be a light sleeper in order to thrive in a profession where things could turn upside down in a minute.

Knuckles to the door, he hesitated. There was no light except the silver glow of the moon flowing up the stairwell. He felt again the ripples of unease, which cascaded along his spine like dissonant notes.

Downstairs.

He descended the creaking staircase, keeping to the edges, where the old wood was least likely to squeal, until he heard a thud and a gasp. After tearing down the stairs, he erupted into the kitchen. Moonlight traced the bulky form of a stocky man bending over something on the floor. Shannon! His breath caught, and he dived forward, slamming the guy against the cupboards.

The man Jack knew as Cruiser rolled quickly, his leather jacket squeaking under Jack's fists. He grunted, wrestling Jack underneath him, until Jack forced him back and off. Cruiser was strong, but Jack was built for long, hard days working two-thousand-pound horses and managing the sprawling family acres. Cowboy tough beat biker muscle any day.

They both shot to their feet. He tried to get a sense of Shannon's condition. She was somewhere in the shadows, but he dared not take his eyes off Cruiser.

"Shan?" he said. "Are you okay? Answer me."

"Ain't this cute? Hubby to the rescue," Cruiser said, pulling a knife from his pocket. Jack knew knives, and he knew fighting, thanks to his brother Owen's sometimes painful lessons. No matter how good your skills were, in a knife fight, you were going to get cut. Period. He pulled a chair close to him and held it up. He considered shouting an alarm, but adding Hazel and Oscar to the mix would elevate the stakes even more.

Keep the knife away from Shannon.

"Shan?" he called again. He thought he heard movement this time, but he couldn't be sure.

Cruiser cocked his head, a grin splitting his face. "You're some tough guy, huh, Cowboy?"

"Come at me with the knife, and you'll find out."

Cruiser's brow creased in thought. "I think we'll have to postpone this little dustup. I've already overstayed my welcome. I'm sure you got plenty of nosy cops in this Podunk town, and killing one will just cause a fuss. Don't you worry, though, Cowboy. I'll be back, and I will shred this inn and anyone in it to find the girl who busted up our boy T.J. and bring his baby home."

"Told you before—there's no girl, not here."

"My informant thinks differently."

"And who's that?"

"None of your business."

Now there definitely was movement at his feet. Shannon got to her knees, surging into the circle of moonlight. She had a coffee mug in her hand and threw the thing as hard as she could. Unfortunately, her aim was off. Jack shifted the chair to protect his head as the cup smashed into the legs, showering him with shards of ceramic.

Cruiser busted out in a guffaw. Jack used the moment to charge toward him, chair first, but he dodged back easily. There was a sound of pounding footsteps, and Oscar barreled into the room, a rifle in his grip.

Cruiser bolted out the door, with Jack on his heels. He would have given anything to have his rope with him to lasso the guy, but skilled as he was, that was a tall order while running barefoot over the gravel. Cruiser had his escape plan ready. A motorcycle was parked on the grass. Cruiser leaped on, kicked the engine to life and sped away.

Biting back the rage, Jack returned to the kitchen. All the lights were on now, and both Hazel and Oscar were crowded around Shannon. Her eyes were huge, the fear rapidly retreating in favor of anger. Nostrils flared, she gathered her robe around her. Anger. Good. He let out a breath.

"Who does he think he is?" she snapped.

"I called Larraby," Oscar said to Jack. "He's on his way."

Shannon avoided her mother's questions. "How'd he find us? Did the person you spoke to on the phone tell him?"

Jack realized his hands were balled into fists, so he forced them to relax. "He's got an informant. Someone close."

Hazel took Shannon's arm. "Please, sit down, honey. He hurt you."

"I'm okay, just winded." She fingered the imprint of Cruiser's arm on her throat.

Rage kindled in his belly, deep down, a foreign feeling. He stalked to the window, looking out on the serene pastures that surrounded the inn. Images shot through his brain, the squeak of leather, the tang of sweat, glint of a metal blade. Violence brought home to people who did not deserve it. It boiled his blood.

Cruiser thought he could roll into town and assault Shannon? Terrorize her into giving up Dina's location or handing Annabell over?

Ain't this cute? Hubby to the rescue.

Jack's marriage had ended almost as soon as it began, but at that moment, in the chilly kitchen, he thought he understood what a husband must feel when his wife was under attack. It was a primal, roaring fire that threatened to explode into a conflagration. He could not explain it if someone paid him to. He breathed hard, fighting for control.

She doesn't want to be your wife, Jack, not really. It's just a charade.

At that moment, it did not matter. His ring was on her finger, and pretense or not, he would make his stand against Cruiser and the Tide.

Shannon's throat pulsed with pain, but she did her best to soothe her mother and convince her uncle to put down the rifle. Oscar left to reassure the guests who had called down to the front desk to ask about the noise.

Shannon thought about Dina, who was running for her life somewhere out in the darkness, desperately hoping her brother would help her.

She closed her eyes, lost in a memory of another day when she'd lived in that very same inn at seventeen years old, waiting for the front door to open or the phone to ring. *Daddy loves you*, her mother said. *He'll come back.*

Daddy doesn't love anybody, she'd come to realize. He needed adoration, his wife's, his daughter's, his mistress's. Their role was to be the mirror that reflected back to Hal Livingston what he wanted to see.

"Hey." Jack touched her shoulder, and she whirled toward him.

"You scared me."

"I'm sorry." His eyes flicked to her neck. Her heart beat hard as he skimmed his calloused fingers along her throat. "You should get that looked at."

She waved him off. "I'm a doctor. Don't you think I'd know if I was seriously hurt?"

"Doctors are the worst patients, so I've been told." There was no smile on his face.

"No, cowboys are."

"Then it's a good thing I didn't let you clobber me with the coffee mug."

That deadpan delivery of his. Now she smiled, and so did he. "Throwing isn't my thing. You know I never hung out on a sports field."

"Except when you took your nose out of a book long enough to watch me run track."

"I was doing my part for the home team."

"Always had my best times when you were there." He looked as though he wished he had not said it, his gaze dropping to his feet. Part of her wished he hadn't, either.

He cleared his throat. "Larraby will be here soon. He'll press for protective custody for you and the baby. He'll be right."

"No."

"Dina's not telling you the whole story about her brother."

"I know."

Chin cocked, he stared at her. "Why are you trying so hard for her, Shan?"

Shan. Why did her nickname sound so soft on his lips? Like they were still a couple.

"I love you, Shan, and you love me, too. Marry me."

And she had, and her soul had found happiness for the first time in her life, until reality set in. They'd had the world at their feet, but they were different worlds. He wanted this world, small town, close family, simple life. She wanted to escape to the big city, climb the career ladder and prove to herself and everyone else that she was the best in her field. He was waiting for an answer. Why was she risking it all to help Dina? "I'm a…"

"Don't give me the doctor-responsibility line."

"It's not a line," she snapped.

He moved closer, boxing her in. "Tell me the truth. Why are you willing to risk your life for Dina Brown?"

She could not look away from the brilliant blue eyes, so insightful and filled with that easy confidence that came from having a stable family who showed you what unconditional love meant. Wrapped up safe in a small town. *You made your choices, Shannon.* She set her shoulders and pushed at his arm. "I'm going to take care of her, Jack, that's all. If you're certain I'm making a mistake, go back to the ranch. There's no reason to continue this marriage farce, even if it amuses you to torture me."

He took her wrist and pulled her a step closer. Her pulse thrummed in her ears. His mouth was so close to hers, and his voice hard and smooth at the same time. "None of this amuses me."

She wanted to fire off a glib retort, something scathing, with snap. But she found she could not utter a word. He leaned in as if he would whisper in her ear, but he said nothing, and neither did she, frozen in the grip of their private thoughts.

For a split second, she wanted nothing more than for him to cross the distance between them, to circle her in strong arms that would stave off the fear, press her against his chest so she could hear the slow and steady beat of his heart. Her mouth went dry, and she stepped back.

"I… I need to check on Annabell."

He released her without another word.

She fled into the room, listening to the sound of his footsteps fading away. Annabell was breathing deeply, lying on her back, with one bitty fist crammed in her mouth. Shannon felt a surge of anger at herself. How had she gone downstairs without her phone, which was, at that moment, across the room, charging next to the bed? How stupid. No, not stupid, she corrected. She hadn't fully understood the stakes.

Now she did. Cruiser impressed that on her. Life or death.

Fine. She was used to those stakes. In the ER, she battled against death every moment of every shift, and most of the time, she won. She'd win this time, too. She reached out to feel Annabell's hands, to be sure the baby was warm enough, when the doorknob rattled. She froze.

Jack? But he would have knocked. As would her mother or uncle. Again the metal handle rattled. A guest? But there were no other rooms on this end of the inn, only hers and the room Oscar was sharing with Jack.

She debated going to grab her phone, but another sound blew all her plans away. It was the sound of something metal sliding into the lock. Not a key, no—more like a file.

Someone was picking the lock.

Phone or baby?

She had only a moment to decide. With a rush of adrenaline, she scooped up the sleeping baby and ran for Night's Stay.

FIVE

Jack heard Shannon scream as he was halfway down the stairs. This time, he bolted up the stairwell. His stomach dropped to find the door unlocked. How stupid he'd been not to know that Cruiser had brought help.

"Shannon," he shouted. She wasn't there, and he was about to check under the bed and in the bathroom when he saw that the door to the adjoining room was open. He grabbed a decorative metal tray from the bureau, crouched low and sped through in time to see Viper's feet vanishing out the open window.

He dropped the tray and grabbed for the boots, but Viper had already dropped to the roof below and hurtled off the edge, sprinting away into the woods. Had he been carrying Annabell? Skin cold with terror, he turned around.

"Shannon?" he called. There was no answer, but the primary door was still bolted from the inside. She hadn't fled that way. Had he missed her in the Garden Room? Nerves iced over, he almost hurtled through the adjoining door when he heard a muffled voice.

"Jack?"

Wildly, he scanned the room. "Where are you?" he bellowed.

Another muted reply, and now he was on his knees, pawing at the bedspread, pushing aside the curtains.

A knock from the middle of the floor. The faint wail of an infant.

His brain scrambled to figure it out.

"Shannon, where?" He was shouting now, and he didn't care whom he awakened.

Again came the thump, but this time, he felt it in his palms, which were pressed flat to the wood floor. Following the steady thumping, he crawled until his knees were directly above the vibration. He slid his fingers over the floor until he found the divot, which could easily have been a simple chip in the wood. In a moment, he'd flung open the trapdoor.

Shannon looked up at him from about four feet down, eyes huge, holding Annabell. "I wasn't sure...at first. I mean, I thought you might be Viper."

"Where are you standing exactly?" he asked through the waves of relief that crashed through him.

"There's a secret room on the first floor. No doors or windows. Some of the miners carried a lot of gold, and they wanted it secured." She quirked a grin. "Occasionally, they needed to hide, also."

He tossed an offended look at her. "You never told me about any secret room."

"A girl has to have some secrets to herself. Here, can you take Annabell, and then give me a hand out? There's a little ladder, but I can't manage it with her."

He reached down and took the baby, hoisting the wriggling bundle and putting her to his chest.

"Hey, Little Bit. You had some adventure, didn't you?" He rocked her, while Shannon climbed out. Her hair was mussed. He could not help himself. He roped her to him with his free arm, inhaling the scent of her shampoo and the musk of the secret room.

"Don't ever do that again, okay?" he breathed.

"What? Outsmart a biker with my keen intellect and problem-solving skills?"

He laughed, long and hard. "You're beginning to sound like me."

"That'll be the day."

"Let's go downstairs. Larraby should be arriving soon."

"Okay," she said, "but you get to do the 4:00 a.m. feeding."

"I think I can handle that."

Shannon and Jack, with Annabell in tow, arrived in the kitchen just as Larraby came through the door. Shannon related the narrow escape to her mother and uncle.

Oscar pawed his beard. "Who would have thought that old trapdoor would come in handy? I meant to nail it up ages ago."

"I'm glad you didn't," she said. "I don't like to think how it would have ended if Viper cornered us before we were hidden."

Larraby held up a hand as Oscar started to reply. "Hold on. Before we get into the full details of what happened here tonight, there's something you need to know ASAP." He fixed Hazel and Oscar with a look. "Too bad there's a vacancy sign in the window."

"Too bad?" Oscar said. "Why?"

Larraby jerked back the lace curtain. A string of three motorcycles rolled up the drive.

"The Tide?" Shannon breathed.

"No. The advance team for the Aces on their way to Wheels Up, but if they find out the Tide is here, there's going to be a war, and this whole town will be caught in the cross fire."

Larraby's words beat an oppressive rhythm in his brain as Jack did a quick shave and pulled on his boots. Since the inn technically didn't open until 5:00 a.m. for check-ins, they had some time after they finished bringing Larraby up to speed. As Jack predicted, he'd lobbied for protective custody for Shannon and Annabell. Shannon flatly refused, and Hazel stood silent at her shoulder. *Dina needs time, and I promised to give it to her*, she'd insisted. *She doesn't trust the police.*

Jack felt as frustrated as Larraby by the time he left. How exactly were they going to keep Shannon and the baby safe in the hotel when the Tide, and now the Aces, were circling like wolves? He wanted to bring them all back to the Gold Bar, where he knew every inch of land like the back of his hand, but he knew Shannon would veto the idea.

He found Oscar with his arm around Hazel, behind the old-oak front desk. Shannon was filling coffee cups for the early risers, who chatted in the dining room over platters of Hazel's legendary currant scones. He took up a spot near the open French doors, unloading mugs from the tubs and stacking them neatly on the table for the later arrivals. This gave him an optimal position to see what would unfold as the Aces arrived.

At the stroke of five, the door creaked open, and three bikers walked in, wearing Ace patches on their sleeveless leather vests. Two were men, broad as barn doors, with muscular arms made in the gym. The other was a woman, small and lean, her curly hair tied behind a green bandanna.

The taller man spoke first. "Need a couple of rooms."

Hazel swallowed. Oscar tightened his grip. "Sorry. We don't have anything available."

The man's thick eyebrow winged up. "Sign says vacancy."

"We've had to close a couple of the rooms to clean the carpets." Oscar shrugged. "Mold."

The woman with the bandanna smiled, but her eyes were cold. "Let's cut through the chitchat. We know we have a reputation, and you're scared of us. Don't feel bad. Everyone is, but we're not here for trouble. Just passing through on our way to Wheels Up, checking out the town for our family. I looked into the end room over there, and it's empty. Looks like it's got two twin beds and a sofa. Plenty of places to crash." She smiled. "Hardwood floors, too, so you won't be needing any carpets cleaned."

Oscar huffed out a breath. "We have the right to decide who's going to stay on our property."

The two men eased forward, their bellies pressed against the shiny wood. Jack tensed, putting down the mugs.

The taller one toyed with a lighter. Hazel stared at it, as if in a daze, while the man spoke.

"Our brothers are rolling through at the end of the week, and we wouldn't want to tell them this was a town filled with unfriendly folks. Aces have long memories."

Jack stalked through the door. "Is that a threat?"

All three stared at him. The woman laughed. "No, it's a deal. You give us a room, and you get no trouble. Refuse us, and bad things will happen."

Jack tried to contain the ire stampeding around his belly. In the herd, there was always a dominant horse, strong, quick to kick or bite the submissives to keep them in their place. These three were all posture and pretense. No way was he going to let them intimidate good people like Oscar and Hazel.

He eyed the patch on the woman's vest. "'Property of Pinball'? You consider yourself property, then?" The thought revolted him.

She glared and tipped her chin up. "I belong to Pinball because I choose to."

When had the world gotten so mixed up that a woman would actually choose to be a man's property? His own mother would laugh herself silly over that notion. He couldn't even imagine what Shannon would say, and he didn't dare turn around to catch her expression.

The tall man clapped her on the shoulder. "Let's go, Tiffany. They've made their choice."

He continued to fidget with the lighter. "I heard there were a couple of bikers in town last night."

"Yeah? Who'd you hear that from?" Jack said.

"Don't matter, just so you know the Aces own this part of the world."

Jack stood taller. "You don't own squat, here."

The guy's face went white. "Anyone showing their colors in this town is a dead man."

Tiffany laughed. "No one would dare, Donny."

Donny returned Jack's hard stare. "Heard it might have been the Tide."

Tiffany blinked, her mouth forming an O-shape of surprise. "No way. What would they be doing on our turf?"

"Waiting to die, I guess," Donny said, his gaze detaching from Jack and drifting across the room to Shannon, who was refilling cups. Jack could tell she was listening in on the conversation. The tremble in her hand gave her away. Could Donny tell also?

The three meandered to the door. Donny tapped his lighter on the tabletops along the way. "Too bad we couldn't come to an agreement." He stopped and flicked the trigger a few times, the little flame dancing and retreating.

"Wait," Hazel called after them.

They turned.

"You can have the end unit. That's all."

Oscar gaped. "But…"

Donny nodded. "Smart choice. We got something to do, and then we'll be back to check in." With one more taunting glance at Jack, he led the way out, and they left, chuckling.

Shannon joined Jack and Oscar, who were staring at Hazel. Without a word, Shannon took her mother's plump hand.

Jack gaped. "Why did you rent them a room?"

"I have to," Hazel mumbled.

"That's crazy. You can't let them stay here, Mrs. Livingston."

"Yes, she can." Shannon's tone was fierce. "The Aces aren't after us, and maybe they can keep the Tide away."

He tried to decipher it all. "But…"

"Stop it, Jack."

There was more. Much more, but it was not the place, so he swallowed his question and closed his mouth.

"When I go upstairs, I'll tell Marie to get the room ready for them, okay, Mom?"

Hazel nodded. "I didn't want to…" Tears shimmered in her eyes.

Shannon pressed a kiss to her cheek. "None of that." Her tone was bright, forced. "You run an inn, right? Can't go around turning down paying customers, can you?"

Jack raised an eyebrow.

"There's no more to be said." Shannon fired

the words at him like arrows as she stalked to the stairwell. "I'm going to check on the baby. I asked Marie to watch her for a while, but now she's got to go prep the room."

Jack hustled to catch her as she climbed the stairs. He heard Annabell's muffled gurgle.

"What's going on?" he demanded, before she could disappear into her room.

"Nothing but the obvious."

"No games, Shannon. I'm serious."

"Do I look like I'm not?"

She looked breathtaking with her hair in disarray and the gold of her irises kindled to flame.

Something deep inside his soul flickered to life, too, and it was a flame he had to douse. Pronto.

He took a breath and tried again. "I need to know what's going on, and you need to tell me. Now."

He'd said his piece, and now he could only play the wait-and-see game.

Waiting for Shannon.

Just like I've been doing all my life.

Shannon knew from the stiff line of Jack's shoulders that she was not going to put him off with her take-charge, emergency-room demeanor. He was not an orderly to be given directives. She'd only managed to boss him when he allowed it. It was one of the things she loved about him and would never in a million years admit. She blew out a breath.

"This inn means everything to my mom. My great-grandfather bought it. It's the only thing she has left, and we almost lost it before, during my senior year."

He folded his tanned arms and listened in that intense way he'd always had, as if every syllable that came from her mouth was golden.

She fought back the beginning of tears. *Don't you dare cry, Shannon.* "The inn was struggling, and my father's newest investment business was tanking, though he only admitted it when his car was repossessed. He was looking for a way out, and the inn was heavily insured."

Something stirred in the oceanic depths of his eyes. More silent listening.

She tried to clear the stubborn lump from her throat. "Dad figured if the inn were to burn down, the insurance payout would fix everything. Mom said no, one of the only times I can recall she ever did to him. No. She shouted it, screamed it at him. I can still hear it when I close my eyes."

Jack's mouth twitched, and she found herself saying the rest. "Dad decided to burn it down anyway. We found him getting ready to set the match to the gasoline. I... I stopped him." There. She'd said it. Finally.

It was as if she was remembering a snippet of a movie from someone else's life. In jerky slow motion, she saw herself racing for the shotgun in the hall closet. Tears streaming. *"Stop, Daddy. Stop, or I will shoot."*

He'd laughed, until the first blast whistled over his shoulder, the shot hammering her eardrum with the force of a pneumatic drill.

"Think about what you're doing, Shannon. I'll never come back if I leave now," he'd said. *"Never."*

A chill crept up her body at the memory.

"I won't let you do it, Daddy. I can't." She realized Jack was still staring at her. "He dropped the match and left for good. Mom and I put it out ourselves."

He reached out those long fingers as if he would touch her. "I remember there was a small fire. Why didn't you tell me?"

Her smile was shaky. "Now, what girl would like to tell her boyfriend about that kind of sordid detail?"

His tone was tender as a spring morning. "The kind who trusts him."

"This isn't about you, Jack."

He exhaled slowly. "You're right. I'm sorry."

"It's okay. My past has made me strong and

determined. I'm not the type to blubber over it."
Infuriatingly, her throat clogged anyway, tears
threatening to undo her bold speech. She shook
her head to clear it. "That's water under the
bridge, but the inn…it's everything. Do you…
can you understand that?" She could not hide
the break in her voice.

He reached for her as if there was no legacy of
pain between them and enfolded her in his arms.
She could not turn away. The muscled feel of
him was familiar, even after so many years, as
if a part of her would always belong with Jack
Thorn. It unsettled her and set her senses reeling.

"I understand." He tipped her gently from side
to side, like there was silent music playing that
only he could hear. "And Donny's threat with the
lighter scared your mother. And you," he murmured into her hair.

"I wasn't scared," she said into his shirtfront.

She felt the rumble of a laugh in his chest. "I
know, Shan. You're never scared."

Yes, I am. She pulled away, searching. "What
about you? Never scared?"

"Been scared plenty."

"I hate the feeling, hate it. What's the cure?"

She could not look away from the silky smile.
"God's got this, like He has every moment of
our lives."

God, the phantom cure-all, the great, invisible fixer in the sky. Backing out of his arms, she shook her head. "You may see evidence of God in your life, but He's nowhere in mine. Never has been. As I've told you, I believe in science."

"They're not mutually exclusive."

"They are for me." She straightened her hair to give her hands something to do, wondering how in the world she'd come to be spilling her guts about her father and talking about God in the stairwell with Jack Thorn, wearing his wedding ring, no less.

The baby's cries grew louder.

"I need to go relieve Marie."

Now his smile was teasing. "Know a lot about babies, do you?"

"I babysat once." And the infant had screamed so loud and so long, she'd deposited it in the crib and called her mother for help within the first hour. "What? I suppose you're an expert?"

He shrugged. "I know a thing or two. I've got bushels of cousins."

The baby's wails reached screech level. *Fussy* didn't quite capture it.

"I'll talk to you later," she said.

He headed for his own room, his long legs eating up the hallway.

She unlocked the door. Annabell's small form was tense, tiny fists clenched and spasming in the uncoordinated way of infants.

"I can't seem to soothe her," Marie said, gray frizzy hair framing her face. "I guess maybe I'm rusty."

"No problem. I'll take it from here. We've got some guests checking in, so Mom needs your help."

After Marie left, she went to the baby and patted her gently on the tummy, inserting the pacifier, which Annabell promptly spit out. She checked the diaper, noted the still-warm bottle on the nightstand, half-full. She put it to Annabell's lips, but she jerked her head away, skin dusky with screaming.

"Easy does it. Your mama should be back anytime now."

Stroking the baby with one hand, she checked her phone messages with the other, her heart sinking as she read the one from Dina.

Haven't found him yet. Still looking.

She texted back. How much longer?

Soon. I promise. Keep her safe. She's all I have.

Breath gone shallow, she texted Jack.

SIX

Shannon was relieved when Jack made it to her room. "What'd the text say?"

She thrust her phone at him. "'Soon.' What does that mean?"

"Means as soon as she can. Don't see why you're all fired up."

"Why am I all fired up?" Shannon's ears vibrated with the baby's shrieks. Such enormous volume from a set of lungs that could only process fifteen milliliters of air per minute. "Because I don't know how to take care of babies, and I panicked," she all but shrieked.

He had the audacity to laugh, so she turned away, resisting the urge to sock him one. "You're a doctor," she muttered under her breath, regretting her decision to text him. "You know all about infant anatomy and behavior. Now go fix the problem." She'd practically brought babies back to life after horrendous car accidents, sustained their fragile vitals until specialists could be summoned. Once she'd even delivered a baby on the floor of the hospital elevator.

Pulling in a deep breath, she gathered up the creature, stunned again at the unsubstantial heft, six pounds, maybe seven, no more. She put the baby to her shoulder and patted her back. Still, Annabell screamed, hot tears squeezing from between her tightly closed eyes, mouth open, pink and wide, as a baby bird's. Her doctor brain supplied the glaring message in spite of the din. "She feels warm to me."

Jack acknowledged with a nod. "I'll phone Mom to get the name of the new pediatrician in town."

The back patting did no good, so she switched to rocking the baby in her arms the way she'd seen the nurses do during her pediatric rotation. This only succeeded in ratcheting up the screaming. Weren't women supposed to be wired to know how to soothe babies? It was a crazy notion, that just because a human happened to have a uterus, she would automatically know how to tend a baby. She scanned her brain for any scant memory left over from her long-ago medical-school textbooks about how to quiet a colicky infant. Nothing. Her memory was normally infallible. Now twinges of panic rippled through her. *This is why you're not sure you ever want one of these, remember?*

Jack disconnected. "Mom's going to text back in a minute," he said over the screaming, thrusting out his arms.

Shannon was only too happy to bundle the baby into his care.

Jack draped Annabell, tummy down, over one of his forearms and gently sandwiched her with the other. He started to sing a song about a horse trotting over grassy green hills with a tot in the saddle. The lyrics were ridiculous, the tune simple, the results jaw-dropping.

Annabell stopped crying.

"How…?" Shannon gaped at him. "How did you do that?"

His smile was sugar sweet. "Told you. I have a way with children."

She did not even try to hold back her laugh.

Crooning and rocking, he swept the baby near his chin, planting a kiss on her downy head. The sight of Annabell's fragile form tucked up next to the strapping cowboy struck at her, a visual reminder of the uncrossable chasm between them. Jack Thorn was meant to be a parent, and she was not sure she would ever be. Never would she want to disappoint a child the way her father had.

Not a surprise, nor a revelation, but a pain lodged fresh under her breastbone. She turned from the tender scene and dumped out the bottle and washed it. Then she folded the baby blanket tossed on the sofa and paced a few circles on the floor.

"Jack, what are we going to do?"

He interrupted his singing, but his steady rocking never waned. "Take care of her." *What else would we do?* his tone implied.

Shannon stared. "For how long?"

He shrugged. "Long as it takes."

The situation was slipping further and further out of her control. She went hot inside, uncertainty turning to irritation. "I didn't sign on for this, Jack. I'm a doctor. I've got a career to take care of. I went out on a limb, stuck my neck out for Dina, and she bolted. How could she do that?"

"She was scared."

"It's no excuse for bad parenting."

"She's barely a grown-up. She panicked. We'll find her, and in the meantime, we'll take care of Annabell."

So calm, as if he was discussing saddles and the cost of feed. She stared him down. "I can't take care of a baby. I'm only off for a short time. I need to get back to my practice. The police…"

He stared right back at her. "You know what

will happen if we turn Annabell over to the police."

She did know. Foster care. The steam leaked slowly out of her. "Jack," she murmured, "I don't think I can do this."

He repositioned the now-calm infant, cuddling her to him. The baby nestled in his arms. She was so small against his wide chest, one tiny hand splayed out, fingers skimming his chin. "You're a strong girl, Little Bit." His eyes were luminous pools. "Let's give Dina a couple of days. We can handle baby care that long, right?"

What do you mean "we"? "We'll need to get a nurse or something."

"Now, how would that look? Little Bit's supposed to be ours, remember?" He pointed to her wedding ring.

Ours. The room was spinning around her. Jack. A baby. Ours. He'd even nicknamed her. When the panic was about to break loose, her mind clung to four words: *a couple of days.* That was all. Seventy-two hours, tops. By then, Dina would have found her brother, and this marriage and motherhood farce would be over.

"I think you're right," Jack said. "She does feel warm. I just got a text, and I'm sure it's Mom. I'll make a doctor appointment." He made to hand her the baby.

"Oh, no," she said, taking out her own phone.

"You keep the baby and tell me the number. I'll call."

"Sure thing," he said, loping off on another round of rocking and singing.

Jack exulted with a fist in the air as he finally wrangled the car seat into place in the back seat of the SUV. It had required twenty minutes and two YouTube videos, but he was satisfied that at long last he'd gotten the thing installed properly. Building the new barn had been easier. He was relieved that Shannon was inside, packing a diaper bag for Annabell, instead of witnessing his aggravation. Her tension was crackling like a high-strung mare's, and he was determined to be calm.

Would Dina really return in a couple of days? What if the Tide found her first? And could Shannon survive the maternal charade he'd forced her into with his lie? He had no answers, only prayers: safety for the women and baby, a prison sentence for Cruiser and courage for himself to fight down the longing Shannon brought to his door the moment she'd called him.

I know I don't have the right to ask, but I need your help, Jack. Man, but it felt good to know she needed him. Though he couldn't be the love of her life, he could show her that being in Gold Bar wasn't the prison she thought it was.

The harder he'd tried to hold on to her, to convince her he could make her happy in Gold Bar, the more she'd wanted to get away. The cool air carried the scent of new grass, the promise of a long, lazy summer, filled with homemade peach ice cream and stargazing at night. She could have been a doctor right here in Gold Bar, couldn't she? Or in nearby Rock Ridge, a city with plenty of people in need.

His thoughts convicted him. *She didn't just want to escape Gold Bar, Jack. She wanted to get away from you. You tried to capture her, hold her in place with a marriage, and that was wrong.*

He swallowed the bitterness as he watched Shannon clomp out the front door, carrying the baby and a bulging diaper bag. He hastened to grab the bag, but she handed over the baby instead.

He managed to get Annabell clipped in the car seat without pinching anything. She set up a wailing that bounced off the windows as he slid behind the wheel.

Shannon leaned against the headrest. "I have a new appreciation for my mother."

"Me, too. And my mom managed to survive three infants, plus Keegan later on, and he was way more trouble than a bushel of babies."

She raised an eyebrow. "Not like his model of an older brother?"

Jack offered mock offense. "I was a perfect child. Ask anyone."

He'd expected teasing, but her expression was sincere.

"Yes," she said, "you have a good heart, always have."

He tried for another joke. "Our high-school principal wouldn't have agreed."

"He doesn't know what you did for me."

Jack would never forget that night, three weeks before graduation. It had been a tumultuous evening with an honor ceremony for which her father had not shown, nor even called, while her mother was admitted to the hospital with an infection. At the teen party, at a mutual friend's house afterward, Shannon had brought in a bottle of whiskey against his protestations. There had been something wild in her eyes that night, something broken and unfixable. Though he hadn't had so much as a sip of the alcohol, he recalled the moment when they'd been found out. He'd hurried Shannon out the back door before he returned to take responsibility for the booze. The admission resulted in his suspension from school and exclusion from the graduation ceremony. He'd never told anyone the truth, but he suspected his parents knew.

Doesn't seem like you, son, he remembered his father had said, eyes probing.

Jack had remained silent.

Sometimes protecting someone from their mistakes doesn't pay in the long run, his father had insisted.

More silence.

Jack knew his father had been right, but he would have done it again to spare her pain and embarrassment. Anything for Shannon. He'd been a fool, sacrificing his own reputation to save hers, a woman who would later shatter his heart. If only he'd known then what he knew now.

Somehow, he figured he would have done exactly the same thing.

I'm a fool.

A grade-A fool.

He drove to the small building sandwiched in between a boarded-up tire shop and a candy store owned by Val, a woman who had known his mother since their grade-school days. The store window was festooned with gold boxes of decadent truffles and hand-sewn bunnies to advertise Val's Hopping Into Spring Sale.

He decided right then and there to buy a box of chocolates after the appointment. Shannon was a chocolate fanatic, and she could use some

soothing since the baby had not stopped screaming all day. And a bunny. He'd get one of those
stuffed bunnies for Annabell. Little girls needed
toys to cuddle—that much he knew for certain.

Along the way, he checked frequently in the
rearview mirror.

Shannon stiffened as a motorcycle rumbled
by. The man behind the handlebars was hairy,
but he was wearing a regular T-shirt with no
gang colors. He bobbed his chin at them as he
passed.

"Barry," Jack said with relief. "Eats at the
Sunrise Cafe every morning."

She didn't reply.

"No one is following us," he reassured her.

"Why do I feel like I'm a rabbit alone in the
open?"

"Only for a few days, and you're not alone."

Though she might prefer to be, he thought.
Well, neither one of them had exactly chosen
this oddball scenario. Finally he pulled into a
parking place in the back lot and hustled to open
the door for Shannon. She didn't wait, instead
jumping out and extracting Annabell from the
seat by herself.

Jack followed them in with the diaper bag over
his shoulder. He knew his brothers would tease
him endlessly, but for some reason, it did not feel
at all awkward toting the pink bag emblazoned

with teddy bears. If girl babies needed pink bags with cartoon animals on them, so be it.

Laura, the nurse, started when she saw them. "Well, hello. It's so good to see you." She did not look as though she meant it.

They had all gone to high school together, and Jack and Laura had even gone out on a couple of dates before he met Shannon. She'd called him a few times in the years after he and Shannon had separated. He'd not returned any of the calls, and eventually she'd stopped trying to contact him. Until his paper marriage was shredded, he would not date anyone else. Had Shannon followed the same rules? Imagining her with another man felt like barbed wire in his gut.

What does it matter now? Still, the thought burned.

Laura clicked some keys on her computer. "I couldn't believe it when I heard you returned, Shannon, with a baby, yet. You're married, you two? I had no idea."

"Yes," Jack said. He looped an arm around Shannon and the baby. "We're married."

Laura's eyebrows quirked as she looked at Shannon. "And you've decided to come home and settle down?"

Shannon colored the tint of a strawberry milkshake. "No, just here temporarily. I'm returning to my internship in Los Angeles very soon."

Confusion played out all over Laura's face. Her calculating gaze slid to Jack. "So, you're all moving then?"

"Lots of details to work out, yet," Jack said, gaze flicking around the space. "Nice office. You like the new doc?"

Her look went all business. "He's very competent. As a matter of fact, he's from Southern California, as well."

The nurse led them back to a small office, which was decorated with jungle animals. A small window showed a slice of the side alley that looked out on the rear of the candy-shop property. A picture of a man, presumably the doctor, with his arms around two teen girls, adorned the wall. They were carbon copies of their father, same stocky frames and wide smiles.

"I'm Dr. Peters," a middle-aged man said as he entered the room and offered his hand.

They shook. "Jack and Shannon Thorn," Jack said. "And this is Annabell."

The doctor smiled. "Lovely baby." He glanced at the computer screen while he weighed Annabell and listened to her heart. His gaze lingered just a moment too long. "For our records, what's her blood type?"

"I don't know," Shannon mumbled.

He quirked an eyebrow. "Didn't Laura tell me you're a doctor?"

Shannon's face went dead pale.

Jack offered a smile. "Doc, we'd really appreciate it if you could help us make Annabell more comfortable, figure out what's bothering her. She's been wailing to beat the band all day."

He peered through a scope into her ear. "She's got an ear infection. I'll prescribe an antibiotic." He scribbled on a notepad and handed the prescription to Jack.

"Where did you deliver Annabell, Mrs. Thorn? What hospital? Just curious. I have a lot of contacts down South."

"Uhhh…" Shannon said.

The doctor leveled a look at them both. "I'm going to need you to provide some proof that this baby is yours."

Jack took a breath. "Call Officer Larraby at the police station. He can vouch for us."

Dr. Peters went silent for a moment, considering. "I will do that. Please wait here." He left.

Shannon arranged Annabell's clothing with shaking hands. "He thinks we abducted this baby."

"Larraby will tell him enough to get him off our backs."

"All this lying, it's too much. I can't keep everything straight." She walked nervously to the window. Cruiser's face appeared, leather-gloved hand pressed to the glass.

As Shannon jerked back from the window, Cruiser smiled.

SEVEN

In a matter of moments, Jack had bundled Shannon and Annabell out of the room and into the hallway, heading for the emergency exit. Shannon could hardly draw a breath.

"Get to the truck. We'll phone Larraby." He pushed through the exit door, steering her toward his vehicle. She nearly stepped on his heels when he stopped short, muttering something in a savage tone.

All four truck tires had been slashed.

Boots echoed on cement. Cruiser was coming from around the other side of the building, cutting off their path back into the clinic.

They crouched on their knees behind Jack's truck. "Plan B. Get to the candy shop and call from there. Val's a friend. She'll help you."

She clutched at him with one hand, Annabell pressed to her side with the other. "What are you going to do?"

"Give you time to get away."

"They'll hurt you."

"Shannon, go."

"No, I won't…"

"Stop talking," he commanded.

She wanted to shout at him for ordering her around, but he was pushing her toward the walkway that would lead her to the street. It was the best option. There might be cars passing there, people, the candy shop only yards away.

One final look at Jack. He was sneaking back to the lot, staying behind the cover of cars as best he could. What was he planning?

Just go. Annabell fussed in her arms, and she bundled her closer, hastening along. She was only a few feet now from the corner where the walkway met the street.

A voice stopped her, just around the corner.

"She went out the back." It was Viper. He was between her and the path to help.

"Is Dina with her?" A higher-pitched voice, vaguely familiar.

"No. She must have her stashed somewhere. At the inn, maybe."

Shannon pressed against the wall, and her skin prickled with fear. There was no choice but to lock herself in the truck or reenter the clinic somehow. Annabell thrashed in the blanket, mouth squinched in preparation for a scream.

Moving as quickly as she was able, she crept

toward the back lot, praying the wail would not emerge from Annabell's mouth.

"It's okay," she whispered in the baby's ear. But it was far from okay.

Scanning frantically, she looked for Jack.

No sign of him. She reached for the handle of the passenger-side door.

Cruiser stepped from his hiding place, the row of bushes next to a gray concrete wall. Terror balled up her stomach. She yanked the door open, but he slammed it shut with his booted foot.

"I want Dina Brown. A nurse said they saw you two leaving the hospital together. Where is she?"

Shannon could only hold Annabell close and hope the child could not feel her wildly galloping heart. "I don't know."

"Then we're gonna take a ride, you and me and babykins, and I'm going to hurt you, badly, you understand, until you tell me. I don't think it will take long to break you, you being a brainiac doctor. You're going to tell me what I want to know in short order."

The handle of the truck bit into her lower back.

"Leave me alone, or I'll scream."

"You do that." He leered. "Makes it more fun."

She tried to bolt, but he caught her before

she'd taken a step. She opened her mouth to yell, but he smacked her with a slap that made her vision go fuzzy.

She stumbled back a step, struggling to hold on to Annabell.

There was no place to go, no place to run.

The sound of Cruiser's slap cracked through Jack, loosing something inside that he could not control. He leaped down from his spot on the concrete wall, where he'd been planning his ambush, and landed on Cruiser, sending him sprawling.

"Run," he hollered to Shannon, as Cruiser thrashed and caught him with an elbow. Her eyes blazed with wild fear. He tried to shout to her again, but Cruiser was reaching for his knife, and it took all Jack's power to stop him. They rolled over the gritty asphalt.

Cruiser caught him in the temple with a dizzying blow that knocked him loose, giving the biker time to get to his feet.

"Should've cut you in two when I had the chance," Cruiser said with a grunt. He went again for his knife, but Jack snaked a boot out and caught his ankle, making him stagger. Jack got to his feet. Shannon was gone, and he rejoiced. She'd gotten Annabell out of there. They would be safe.

In the meanwhile, he'd buy them some time. He launched himself at Cruiser again, slamming him back into the wall of the clinic and dodging his wild jabs. Cruiser recovered, and Jack took two punishing blows to the chest. They darted wary circles around each other. Cruiser was wide and muscled, but Jack could dance around the sharpest hooves. Normally Jack could weather any dustup by playing it smart, strategy over brute strength, but now he was angry. The slap on Shannon's face blasted away his sense of caution. It didn't matter that Cruiser shouted to somebody. It wouldn't make a difference if the guy pulled an Uzi from his pocket. He would stop Cruiser and punish him for raising a hand to Shannon.

He shot out his fist, connected with Cruiser's cheekbone and heard the thwack of flesh on flesh. A shadow crept into his vision, and there was a sudden blow to the backs of his shoulders, sending him to the ground in a shower of sparking pain. He had enough left to roll and dodge the second blow. Viper, with a section of steel pipe in his grip, raised his arm to crush Jack's skull. Jack rolled, shoulders bumping against the curb. He had nowhere to go.

He tried to get to his feet, but Viper's next blow landed on his ribs, driving him to ground again.

"Kill him," Cruiser said, panting. "Kill the cowboy right here."

Viper raised the pipe to unleash the death blow. A shot rang out. Both bikers ducked.

"Let's beat it," Viper snarled.

Jack's confused senses registered running feet, a motorcycle engine kicking to life and the purring vibration of the blacktop under his body as they rode away. He should get up, but at that moment, it was all he could do to move air past his teeth and into his lungs.

Shannon threw herself to her knees. "Jack..."

He opened one eye. The other seemed to resist his efforts. "The baby..."

"She's safe with my daughter, back at the candy shop," a familiar voice said. Val peered down at him, her white hair neatly braided and the rifle slung over one shoulder. "Sorry I didn't plug him, Jack. Eyes aren't what they used to be, and I didn't want to risk too much more shooting."

"Good thinking," Jack said, groaning as he tried to sit up.

"Stay still. Let me see how bad it is."

"Not bad," he said, gritting his teeth as Shannon gently pressed on his ribs. "Been through worse."

She huffed out a breath. "Sometimes I think

your hat cuts off the blood circulation to your head. You should have run. Why didn't you run?"

He caught her wrist in his fingers, both to keep her from prodding any more and to reassure himself she was really there. She stilled, and he touched her cheek with his finger, a developing bruise showing from Cruiser's slap. "Can't let anyone hurt my woman." He added a lopsided smile.

"I… I'm not…" Her face went all cotton-candy pink. Her mouth opened and then closed, and she ducked her head. When she finally could look at him again, her eyes blazed molten honey. She leaned close, her hair tickling his forehead, lips grazing his earlobe as she whispered, "I am not your woman, and you will not get yourself killed for a pretend marriage. Do you hear me?"

He closed his eyes and savored the scent of her that momentarily dulled the pain. "Yes, honey-bunch," he said, trying not to chuckle when she pinched his ear. "May I sit up now?"

Shannon eased back. "I don't suppose I'm going to stop you."

"You're not big enough to stop me," he could not resist saying.

The doctor came out, along with his nurse. "The police are coming. Do you need an ambulance?"

"Of course he needs an ambulance," Shannon said. "Look at him."

"Naw," Jack said.

"And of course, he's going to turn his back on any kind of commonsense idea," she said, getting to her feet, "because he's got the brains of an old mule."

"Hey," he said, "smartest beast I ever knew was an old mule. Went by the name of Nacho."

"Come on, then, Nacho," she said with a sigh. "Let's get you to your feet."

His two brothers pulled up in their truck as he managed an upright position, leaning heavily on Shannon's shoulders.

"I asked Val's daughter to call them," Shannon explained.

Barrett hastened over, with Keegan right behind.

"How bad?" Barrett said.

Jack went for a shrug that turned into a grimace.

"I thought Owen taught you how to fight," Keegan said, handing him his hat. "You look like a half-chewed rabbit."

"Thanks," Jack said. He took a breath and pulled away from Shannon. "I'm good. Just need some ice and an aspirin."

"And a CAT scan, X-ray and possibly a couple of sutures," Shannon chimed in. "None of which he will allow, I'm sure."

But Jack wasn't listening. His brothers were

working on moving the baby's car seat to Barrett's truck, while Keegan called a friend who could hook them up with new tires for Jack's vehicle. He stared toward the road where Viper and Cruiser had fled.

They'd be back, he knew.

And now that blood had been spilled, he understood it wouldn't end until one of them was on the ground.

It's gonna be you, Cruiser. You'll never hurt Shannon again.

His promise.

And he would keep it.

EIGHT

How had they known? Shannon alternated between out-and-out terror at what could have happened at the clinic and a burning need to solve the mystery. Cruiser and Viper knew they would be at the clinic with Annabell. Had they been following without Shannon or Jack noticing? Had someone at the ranch heard Evie passing along the number? Or was it a patron at the inn? The three bikers came to mind, but it made no sense that they would tip off their enemy gang. Larraby promised to see what he could come up with. In a small town like Gold Bar, there couldn't be too many places for two bikers to hide.

Shannon and Annabell accompanied the Thorn brothers back to the ranch.

She would have preferred to return to the inn, but Evie had been informed of the attack and would mount a full-out posse if Jack wasn't brought immediately home. Shannon did not want to take her eyes off him, anyway, since he was too hardheaded to seek the proper medical treatment. Hard head, soft heart.

Her stomach tightened as she remembered.

Can't let anyone hurt my woman.

The man was also delusional.

My woman.

Like she was some sort of horse to be owned. It was insulting, she decided, and when he was somewhat recovered, she intended to tell him so.

Keegan arrived with the antibiotics for Annabell, and she attempted to get a dose of the pink stuff down the baby's throat with the plastic syringe. Annabell squirmed and thrashed. The liquid dribbled down her neck and stained her clothes.

"Just one minute is all I need, Annabell," she said. "Come on, sweetie. You can do this." She shot a look at Keegan. "Can you hold her still?"

"Uh, well," he said, backing toward the door. "I gotta go, uh, saddle something." The door bumped closed behind him.

She sighed. "Coward."

"Bring her to me," Jack called. He was lying on his back, on the sofa, with an ice pack on his eye and another on his ribs.

"You're in no condition to help."

His tone was peevish. "Got two arms, don't I?"

Desperate, she carried Annabell to Jack and

nestled her next to him. He cradled her to his side and started to sing the horsey song again, jiggling her softly to the beat of the music. Once again, she quieted, at least enough that Shannon was able to squirt the medicine down her throat.

"I'll sit up in the rocker and hold her," he said, grimacing as he eased upward.

"No, you won't."

"I'm okay. Just give me a minute."

"You are a mess, and you shouldn't be…"

"Jack, listen to Shannon," Evie said as she marched into the room, handing him a fresh ice pack.

"What? You're on her side now?"

"I'm on the side of common sense. Both of you quiet down and give me that baby. We're going to rock on the porch swing until she falls asleep. I've got the portable crib set up in the guest room." With that, Evie took the infant, wrapped her in a blanket and sailed out the door.

Shannon sank into a chair. "We can't go on like this."

"You're right. You should move in here."

She gaped. "What?"

"The inn's not safe. Someone has ears there, figured out we were going to the clinic. You should stay here, at the ranch, in my room." He colored. "I'll sleep in the guest room, of course."

She felt the force of being sucked back into

Jack's orbit, the ranch, his small-town life. Her future in Los Angeles was edging farther away. It wasn't going to happen. "No. I'm fine at the inn with Annabell."

"You're not. It's best for you and the baby here."

"Don't tell me what's best," she said. "You don't have the right."

His gaze raked the ceiling, and she saw him settle into that calm place he occupied when she was at her angriest. "I realize I don't have the right to give you orders, Shan. I'm not trying to do that. I want you and Annabell to be safe. And here, at the ranch, I'm one of four brothers who know how to fight and shoot, not to mention my mom, who is a better shot than all of us."

She didn't want to look at him, to connect with those exquisite blue eyes, so she kept her head down, staring at her fingers, which were twisted together in her lap. A wall of fear and frustration slammed up against her and drove out her last drop of energy. "I'm not part of this world anymore, Jack. Don't ask me to be."

He was silent a moment. "I'm being practical. I told you, I understand this is all pretend. Not trying to rope you here."

"But you did before," she said quietly, finally looking at the cut across the bridge of his nose and the swollen lower lip. "The marriage. You wanted me here with you, and you figured marriage would seal the deal, that I'd come home from med school and settle in Gold Bar."

"It's supposed to seal the deal," he snapped. "Marriage is joining two lives together, and that means living in the same county, at least, doesn't it?"

"It wasn't just about proximity, and you know it. I wanted different things than you, and I still do." She got up and paced. "I want a career that heals people. I want to be the best at what I do, being a doctor. I don't know if I will ever be able to devote enough time for a proper relationship, or children. I told you that right up front."

"I never expected you to give up your career. I'd be willing to leave the ranch, just like I said when we got married, if that's what you needed."

"Leaving Gold Bar would be like cutting off your arm. Why would you agree to that?"

His mouth twitched. "Because I thought you were worth it."

Worth it. An ache started up behind her breastbone, the ache left by her father, whom she could never please, and a town where she would never belong. It was fed by long days, longer nights and years that flew by before she could catch hold of them. "But you don't think so anymore, do you?" she asked.

"Shan," he said, voice barely a whisper. "You're

worth so much more than you can ever imagine, to me and to God."

Tears blurred her vision. "I'm not wife material, and I should never have agreed to get married. It's the worst mistake I ever made. I'm sorry I hurt you. I truly am."

He cocked his head, generating another wince as the movement aggravated some tortured muscle or nerve. "Know what, Shan?"

"What?"

"You're the smartest woman I know, and for all that book learning, you're just plain wrong about the big stuff."

Her mouth dropped open. "Are you trying to make me mad?"

"Nope. Trying to keep you safe. You and Annabell are moving in here tonight because it's the smart thing to do. End of discussion." He grabbed his Stetson from the coffee table, settled back onto the sofa and covered his eyes with his hat. "Been reading this book on babies, and it says the parents ought to nap when the kiddos do. Sounds like a good plan to me."

Reading a baby book? She was rendered speechless.

In a matter of moments, he was breathing deeply, one booted leg crossed over the other, fingers laced across his flat stomach.

"Jack Thorn, you are incorrigible."

She thought she saw the flicker of a smile curve across his lips as he settled deeper into sleep.

Jack knew it was hard for Hazel to have her daughter and temporary grandchild departing for the ranch, but she came around in the end, thanks to Oscar's support.

"We can't keep them safe here, sis, with all the guests milling around." Oscar's thick brows crimped. "Denny, over in Rock Ridge, called and said the Aces have plumb taken over the town there. Headed our way next to get to that Wheels Up event. Larraby's put all his cops on mandatory recall, so it's clear he's expecting trouble."

Hazel clutched her daughter's shoulders. "Be careful. Don't go out anywhere on your own. Promise."

"I promise," Shannon said. "But I hate to leave you with Tiffany, Donny and what's his name here on the property. They're dangerous."

"So far, all they've done is rent a room, but we're keeping a close eye on them. Jack's right. You're going to be safer at the ranch," Hazel said.

Shannon shot him an uncertain look as he tried not to show the pain ricocheting through his ribs and skull. "Only temporary," he said. "Dina should be calling anytime now."

Hazel and Oscar walked them to Jack's truck, which was now sporting a new set of tires. It was pure agony on his ribs to yank open the door for Shannon, but he did. She offered a smile and left him there, snagging the keys from his hand and skirting around to the driver's side.

"Hey," he said.

"You look like you're about to fall over. I'm driving." She climbed behind the wheel, leaving him sputtering like a teakettle on the boil. "Well?" she countered. "Do you need Uncle Oscar to give you a boost, or can you manage to get into the truck on your own?"

Muttering, he climbed into the passenger seat, slamming the door for good measure. Both Hazel and Oscar didn't bother to hide their smiles as Shannon started the engine.

He intended to keep better hold of his keys in the future. Why, he wondered, did she have to look so beautiful along with looking so smug? Still miffed, he tried and failed to find a comfortable sitting position.

They were almost to the narrow exit of the fenced lot when Tiffany stepped out in front of them. Shannon slammed to a halt, and Jack bit back a groan of pain.

Tiffany walked to the driver's side and rapped a knuckle on the window.

"Don't open it," he said.

"It's not like she's going to try anything here," Shannon said, rolling down the window halfway, but keeping the engine running. "What do you want?"

"Heard you were in town, looking for trouble." Her gaze flicked over Jack's battered face, and she grinned. "I see it found you. You land any punches or just take them?"

He didn't rise to the taunt.

She noted the duffel bag sitting between them. "Running, then?"

"We're not running anywhere," Jack said.

"You should. I heard that the Tide thinks you're hiding a girl from them, Dina Brown, and you're keeping the baby for her." She peered into the back seat.

"We're not, but why are you so interested?" Shannon demanded. "What's our business got to do with you?"

"Your business brought the Tide onto our turf. That's gonna start a war with the Aces. Now, I enjoy a good fight, mind you, but Pinball's not gonna back down without blood."

"Your Pinball? The one that owns you?" Jack did not bother to keep the sarcasm from his tone.

"Pinball leads the Aces. He's our general."

Jack leaned forward, and his muscles paid the price. "Tell General Pinball we have nothing to do with Dina Brown or her baby."

"It's not that easy."

He waved an impatient hand. "Speak your mind," he said. "You didn't stop us to chat. Say what you came to say."

Tiffany ran a finger over the window glass, releasing a squeak that set his teeth on edge. "If it's true, and that baby is Dina's, give her to me."

Shannon stared. "You have to be kidding me."

"The baby and the girl belong to the Tide," Tiffany repeated, eyes flat as wet river rock. "But we can hide them until the Tides give up and go home to Los Angeles. No war. No mess. No fuss."

Shannon was openmouthed, mute.

"So, you're here on Pinball's behalf, then?" Jack said, biting back his own fury.

Tiffany shifted. "He doesn't want a war, but that's not for public knowledge."

Jack nodded. "Oh, I get it. Because if it became public knowledge that you were trying to manipulate things, Pinball would look weak, like he's scared to go to war with the Tide."

She slapped a palm on the glass, and Shannon jumped. "He ain't scared of nothing."

"Swell for him," Jack said. "He must be quite a guy. You can deliver a message for me. The baby is ours, end of story. If you mess with our child, you will find out exactly what a war looks like, and it will be the kind of war you cannot win. Do you understand me?"

Tiffany's mouth hardened to a thin line.

"Give Pinball the message," Jack said. "We're leaving now."

Shannon rolled the window up and eased the truck out of the lot. He didn't look in the rearview—didn't have to. Tiffany was still standing there, staring, probably weighing how to communicate their unfriendly message to her boss.

His pulse was tattooing in his ears, and he was hot all over. He rolled down the window to let in the spring breeze, and he sucked in a lungful of it before turning back to Shannon. She was pale, eyes shadowed with fatigue, desperately in need of a good night's sleep.

She'd get it at the Gold Bar.

He reached out and touched her shoulder, massaging gently where her neck met the graceful curve of her collarbone, fingertips feeling the rapid rise and fall of her breathing.

"They really think…these people…they really believe Dina and her baby are property. Property." She turned blazing eyes on him. "I can hardly make myself believe it."

"Me neither." He thought about his words. Had he made her feel like that, too? "You know, when I said that about…about you being my woman, I didn't mean… I know that's not how God meant things between a man and woman to be. I just…"

She shook the hair from her brow. "It was your bravado talking, your stiff-necked cowboy pride. I don't belong to you or anyone else."

He decided silence was the safest avenue to take, but she wouldn't allow it.

"Are you going to say something silly like 'it's going to be okay, Shan'?" she demanded.

"It is."

She sighed, and it came out like a whimper. "I don't want to be in this situation, but I will never give Annabell to the likes of Tiffany or Cruiser. Ever."

The ferocity of it tightened his stomach. Shannon, for all her maddening qualities, was a warrior, through and through.

That's my honeybunch, he thought, finally easing into a comfortable spot.

He surprised her in the wee hours of the morning, somewhere well past midnight and short of sunrise. On his way back from the kitchen to swallow another handful of aspirin, he heard the baby mewling. Wouldn't do him any harm to rock Annabell for a while. He figured he'd tap on the door, and if there was no response, he'd slither in quiet like, pick up Annabell and sneak her to the family room, without waking Shannon. He found she was already up, walking the baby in slow circles around the room, singing something about doctors and thermometers to the tune of his horse song.

She broke off with a gulp when she noticed him.

"Didn't mean to startle you." He grinned. "Nice song, Doc."

The moonlight gilded her smile. "I think she might want to be a doctor when she's not riding horses."

"She might, indeed," he said. They both perused the exquisite profile, delicate forehead and the tiniest fingers that flexed and curled to their own cadence. So perfect, he thought. So fresh from God. His heart swelled.

"Want me to take a turn with her so you can get some sleep?" he whispered.

"No, it's okay. I'm used to the graveyard shift."

"All right, then." He strode over quickly and kissed Annabell's head, soft as bird feathers. Before he knew what he was doing, he kissed Shannon, too, on the temple, where the hair met the satin skin, smooth as moonlight, silken as the sunset. She did not move away, and for a heartbeat, neither did he.

It felt like family for a perfect moment, him and Shannon and the baby.

Until he remembered, with a swift jab to the gut, that it was just pretend, smoke and mirrors.

"Good night, Shannon," he whispered as he left.

NINE

On Saturday morning, Shannon paced laps around the ranch house, walking the baby, feeding and burping her when Evie hadn't staked a claim, and checking in with the hospital. She'd texted Dina repeatedly. The minutes crept by in ultra-slow motion.

While Annabell slept under Evie's watchful eye, Shannon wandered out into the spring sunshine. She figured Jack was probably sleeping late, and he was going to be feeling every bit of damage from his fight with Cruiser.

She could still feel the touch of his finger on her cheek and his kiss to her temple.

Shan, you're worth so much more than you can ever imagine, to me and to God. How lovely and precious it must be to believe those words, but worth was measured by achievement, accomplishment and contribution. Right now, spinning her wheels, she was doing none of those things, and it tortured her. It was well and good that the ranch business kept the Thorns in constant motion, but what about her life? Her internship? Her purpose?

Restlessness kept her walking past the grazing horses with their tails swishing, and she found Barrett in the hay barn, tossing bales down into the bed of his truck.

"Morning," he said. She did not know Jack's older brother well, and his dark beard masked his expression. She was probably not his favorite person after what she'd done to Jack.

"Good morning."

Shelby joined Shannon, handing her a cup of coffee. "Saw you headed here. I just made a fresh pot. Full disclosure—it's decaf, which Barrett won't touch."

"I'd touch it if you made it," Barrett called. "Just wouldn't drink it."

Shelby laughed. "Cowboys. What are you gonna do?"

"I'd love to know the answer to that," Shannon said. "How is the house coming?"

"Done, except for some interior details." She jutted a chin at Barrett. "Hard to get him to talk about tile and such when there's a ranch to run."

Barrett hopped down from the tower of hay and kissed his wife. "I will talk about tile with you all day long, as soon as I get these horses fed."

Shannon felt a swell of envy toward the couple. They were so obviously in love, with their hopes and desires in sync. If only it could be that simple…

"Do you know when Ella and Owen will be back?"

"Next week," Shelby said. "They took Betsy to visit their cousin and they're staying awhile, looking into some building plans of their own. They've got their eye on a property a few miles from here where Ella could house her blacksmith shop and Owen would be only a few minutes from the ranch. Owen's got big plans to make the house completely accessible for Betsy's wheelchair."

Shannon nodded, guilt rising. Ella was her best friend, and she hadn't known anything about her plans. Sucking in a breath, she resolved to change things, to wrestle work back into the space where it belonged.

"Jack's working the new mare in the far pasture," Barrett said. "If you were looking for him, I mean."

Something in his eyes, so like Jack's, made her think he figured she ought to do some patching up with his little brother. Or perhaps, he just wanted to get his new wife all to himself. "He's crazy to be doing anything but resting with his injuries."

Barrett quirked a smile. "With Owen gone,

we're a man short. And anyway, Jack's quieter than the rest of us, but he's not any better at taking orders."

"None of the Thorn brothers are, unless the orders come from their mama," Shelby said with a laugh.

Shannon thanked him and cradled her coffee, absorbing the warmth. As she walked away, she saw Barrett loop an arm around Shelby's waist and draw her close for a lingering kiss. Heaving in a breath, she went to go try to talk some sense into his younger brother.

She found Jack holding the lead rope of a bay mare. He stood close to the animal, stroking a palm over her neck, speaking softly. While she watched, he eased the hand with the rope up to do the neck stroking, and the other rubbed long slow passes onto the horse's nose. In one quick movement, he slicked his nose hand up across the horse's ears. The horse tried to rear back and toss her head, but Jack kept her nose down with gentle pressure. Then it was right back to the neck and nose stroking and quiet talk. She watched in fascination as he repeated the whole procedure half a dozen times, until the horse's reaction to having her ears touched lessened.

"Good girl," Jack said. "You pretty thing. Doing just great."

He finally pushed back his Stetson and caught

sight of her there. He let the horse loose and walked to the fence with only a slight hitch, but he was probably covering. The lines around his mouth were pronounced.

"I suppose that horse couldn't have waited until you're healed for her lesson?"

Jack shrugged. "She's head-shy. Got a bad cut to the ear a month back, and now she's gotten the fear in her. We're being paid to get her past that, and every day we don't work with her is a missed opportunity."

"How many lessons will she need?"

"As many as it takes until she learns to trust that I'm on her side, that I'm not gonna hurt her."

Shannon wondered if they were still talking about the mare.

He looked closely at the bruise on her cheekbone. "Hurt much?"

She shook her head. "How are you feeling? Never mind. You're going to say 'right as rain,' or something macho like that, right?"

"Actually, I feel like I got caught in a stirrup and dragged a hundred acres over bumpy ground." He grinned. "But I wouldn't admit that to anyone except you, on account of you're a medical professional, sworn to secrecy and all that, right?"

She could not help but laugh. "Well, you're not my patient, Mr. Thorn, but I'll keep that in mind." Her eyes wandered over the green fields and the white fences, aglow with spring splendor. Soft sunshine mellowed her tension, warmed her skin. "It's hard to believe."

"What?"

"That there are people in town trying to take Annabell, to capture Dina. People who would beat you bloody." She shook her head. "I shouldn't be shocked by anything after working in an ER—the things people do to each other."

"You've seen the worst, huh?"

"I always think I've seen the worst, and then something else rolls through the door."

"How do you take it?"

She raised an eyebrow. "You really want to know?"

He nodded.

"I remind myself over and over that I was made to heal people. That's all. That's my job, so I do it no matter how awful the case is."

"And it's your calling." His look of admiration made her blush. "I dunno if I ever told you, but it makes me proud to know you're a doctor."

"Really?" His words reached her to the core. Jack was the finest man she knew, and he was proud of her.

"Yes, ma'am. God doesn't fit many to that occupation."

"It wasn't God. It was college and med school and dedication."

"Yeah?" He leaned on the fence, forearms knotted with muscle. "Ever heal someone who shouldn't have made it?"

She flashed immediately on a three-year-old child who was hit by a cab after he wandered away from his mother into the street. He was in terrible condition, massive blood loss and shock, and he shouldn't have lived, but somehow he had. He'd lived and thrived. "Yes. Luck."

That slow smile crept over his face. "Not luck. Your skill, plus God's will. Takes both." He leaned forward and tucked her hair behind her shoulder, making her tingle. "You don't get to save a life without His permission. But to be His partner in that…" He shook his head, eyes blue as the deep sea. "That's something truly special, something to be real proud of."

It had teased through her mind in those long, quiet hours in darkened hospital hallways, gliding past families with clasped hands and mouths mumbling prayers, that there was someone greater than she deciding which lives would continue and which would not. When the little boy had lived, her soul rose up in gratitude, but to what? To whom? Not her skill. Not chance or coincidence. But if God intervened in such magnificent ways, then why hadn't He answered her prayers?

Please make Daddy love me.

Please.

Incomprehensibly, emotion from those little-girl prayers thickened her throat and blurred her vision. *So long ago, Shannon. What's the matter with you?*

Jack did not miss it. He twined his fingers with hers, keeping her from turning away. His touch was steady and warm and wonderful. She found herself dizzied, until she was saved by the buzz of her phone.

"It's a text from Dina," she said, clearing her throat. He exited the pasture through the gate and joined her, crowding close to see the screen. He smelled of hay and horses and spring air. She blinked hard.

"She said everything's okay. She wants us to bring Annabell to meet her at the airstrip this afternoon, at three. I told her about that in the hotel room, how I used to play there as a kid. Just trying to calm her down with anything I could think of."

"Tell her no. The police station, the post office, someplace public."

Shannon typed in the information and sent the text. No reply. She sent another and then called Dina. Still no answer.

"You don't trust her?"

He blew out a breath. "Seems like an odd place to meet to me."

"She's scared of the Tide. Maybe the Aces, too. Maybe, somehow, she's got wind that some of Pinball's people are looking to hand her over to the Tide."

He didn't answer.

"So, what do you think we should do?" Shannon demanded when she could not stand the silence anymore.

"I think we're gonna make plans," he said.

"What kind of plans?"

"The kind you're not gonna like."

TEN

They loaded the car seat into his truck at 2:30 p.m. Barrett had already saddled Titan and departed, and Keegan had gunned his motorcycle to life and headed out a few minutes after Barrett.

Evie stood in the doorway, holding a cell phone. "No word from you boys in thirty minutes, and I change the plan." Her brows were drawn into a thin line. "Seriously, Jack. I'm not kidding."

He didn't need the words to know that. "Yes, ma'am."

Shannon squeezed out the door around his mother.

"No," he said, trying to snag her.

"Yes," she retorted. "You aren't going to look convincing if I'm not there with you. Dina will be scared, if it is her."

"Shannon…"

She was already climbing into the front seat. He strode over and caught her arm.

She shot him a haughty look. "Are you going to manhandle me like a naughty colt?"

"Tempting," he said through gritted teeth. "You're behaving like one."

She wrestled the door from his grip and slammed it. *Get in*, she mouthed through the glass.

He heard a snicker, but when he looked, his mother was the picture of innocence. If his mama and Shannon ever decided to double team him, he had no chance at all. Out of options, he dragged himself behind the wheel and gunned the engine.

They drove for a while.

"Is this your usual silence, or am I getting the cold shoulder?" she said.

"You don't want to hear my thoughts, believe me." He tried to relax his grip on the wheel.

"All right. Change of subject. Are you still wanting to buy my uncle's airstrip?"

He jerked. "How'd you know that?"

That half smile. "I have my ear to the gossip wheel," she said.

"Keeping tabs on me, huh? I'm flattered to no end." He was rewarded with a deep blush that blossomed on her cheeks. He squelched a smile.

"Yeah, I want to buy it. Almost got your uncle willing to let it go."

"He lets you use it, regardless. Why do you need to buy it?"

"A man doesn't like to borrow."

She rolled her eyes and muttered something about cowboys.

"And I like the way it makes me feel, to know I can take off whenever I want to on ranch business…or personal stuff."

She stopped talking then, probably remembering the times he'd flown to Southern California to try to make her talk to him about their sad excuse for a marriage. Or maybe thinking about her desperate call to him that had started the whole crazy adventure in motion.

There wasn't more time to ponder as they drove onto the weed-bordered airstrip and he reduced his speed to a slow roll. There were no cars visible—no people at all, for that matter—only the long strip of asphalt and the ramshackle tower on the far end.

"Is there a back way in?" Shannon said.

"Yeah, a dirt road. Barrett's watching from there."

"Where's Keegan?"

"He'll be around if we need him."

The minutes ticked away, 2:58, 3:00, 3:05. At 3:06, the entrance to the airstrip was crowded by two bikers thundering up the runway. Cruiser and Viper.

Shannon bit her lip. "What have they done with Dina?"

Jack got out and stood by the passenger side, speaking through the open window. "Stay in the truck."

"What if things go bad," she said, her skin gone pale.

He bent to look her full on. "Not gonna let that happen. Now, stay put. I mean it."

For once, she appeared to listen. "Jack, I'm scared. Be careful."

He wasn't scared, but his nerves were jumping as he watched Viper and Cruiser's progress from under the brim of his hat. Shannon had complicated things by coming along against his wishes. It was one thing to wrestle with a treacherous horse, another to do it with a woman right behind you.

They stopped and got off their bikes. Cruiser grinned.

"Awww, what'sa matter, Cowboy? You look kinda banged up. Those bruises getting you down?"

"Where's Dina?"

"Now, that's a good question, but first things first. We want the baby."

Jack let his hands go loose at his sides. Ready. "You're not getting the baby or anyone else."

"I think I am, boy." Cruiser went for the gun at his belt. Jack tensed as a rifle shot plowed into the ground at Cruiser's feet. Cruiser whirled, looking for the sniper, and so did Viper.

From the top of the tower, Jack's dad laid down another perfect shot, which stopped them midtracks. He almost laughed.

"You sent a message from Dina's cell phone. Where is she? What did you do with her?"

Cruiser sneered. "Dunno what message you're talking about. We were out for a ride, weren't we, Viper? Saw you turn in. Wanted to pay our respects."

"You can tell me," Jack said. "Or you can wait for the cops. They should be here soon. Still got a couple of assault charges pending they'd love to talk with you about."

Cruiser sucked in a breath and let it out slowly. "We don't have to get all uppity like. We know that baby isn't yours. It's ours. Hand it over, and we can go our separate ways. The doc there can find some other messed-up kid as her charity project."

He prayed Shannon would not come flying out of the truck in a fit of justified anger at such talk.

In a whirl of motion, Viper pulled his gun and aimed at the truck window, but Jack's dad laid down a volley of shots before he could pull the trigger. Viper and Cruiser bolted for their bikes. Keegan roared up on his motorcycle, intercepting the two before they could climb aboard.

"Can't leave now," Keegan said. "Party's just getting started."

"All right," Jack said. "Now it's time for you to tell us where Dina Brown is."

Cruiser's face blazed hatred in a steady wave. He uttered an expletive and went again for his gun. Again, Tom unloaded a shot, and Keegan kept between the men and their bikes.

"Drop your guns and answer him," Keegan shouted. "I'm wasting gas."

Cruiser spit on the ground. "There's your answer."

Two more shots, one so close it nearly hit his boot, convinced Cruiser to toss his gun to the ground, and Viper followed suit.

The radio clipped to Jack's belt squawked.

"Aces just passed me on their way in," Barrett said. "A half dozen, ready for battle."

Jack's blood turned to ice. "Everybody leaves," he called into the radio, shouting to Keegan. "Get Dad. Get out of here." Keegan immediately gunned it to the control tower. Jack raced to the driver's seat as the Aces rolled onto the tarmac.

They started shooting immediately, aiming for Cruiser and Viper, unconcerned about who would be caught in the cross fire. Bullets slammed into Jack's truck as he sought the ignition.

"Shannon, stay down," he thundered.

The back door of the double cab opened, and Viper was there, yanking at the baby seat. "Stop," Shannon shrieked, slapping at his hands just as a bullet fractured the back window, sending glass rocketing in all directions. Viper recoiled, but only for a moment. Then he lunged again as Jack punched the truck into motion.

"He's in the truck," she screamed. In the rearview, Jack saw Viper attempt to cut through the seat belt with his knife. Shannon screamed again, and Viper tumbled free without his burden. Aces poured onto the runway, blocking his exit.

"Gonna have to get to the trail," he yelled.

Shannon gripped the armrest. He pushed her head down to keep her from the path of the incoming bullets that zinged around them like hornets. Pedal to the floor, he prayed the Aces would be too occupied with Viper and Cruiser to pursue them. Keegan, with his father behind, was already roaring away over the dirt trail.

He pushed the truck as fast as it would go. A biker peeled off in pursuit, coming alongside the driver's door. He held a revolver, struggling to keep it steady and the bike under control. The Aces would try to eliminate witnesses to their shooting rampage, mowing down anyone who could incriminate them. One shot, one wild bullet, could catch Shannon. Stomach doing flips, he jammed the accelerator to the floor, but the biker did not slow.

The biker squeezed off a shot, which exploded his side-view mirror and caused Shannon to scream again. They could not outpace their pursuer, and they would have to slow to make it to the dirt trail without overturning. Shannon gripped the seat belt, knuckles white.

"Keep it steady," he said, gesturing her to grab the wheel.

She must have thought him crazy, and she was probably right, but she took hold of the wheel, keeping the truck on a straight path. Foot still on the accelerator, he used both hands to slam the driver door open with every bit of his strength. As the biker swerved to avoid the door, he jerked the handlebars too hard and overturned the motorcycle.

"Yes," he said, grabbing the wheel again. Shannon let go, panting.

Then they were through the entrance to the trail, bumping over the dirt, the ruts on the path rattling his teeth. Barrett hopped off Titan and closed the gate, padlocking it shut. The Aces might get through it, but it would take a while.

He waited until his brother was back in the saddle and safely away through the woods before he took the trail back home, knowing Barrett or his father had already alerted Larraby.

Shannon still clutched the armrest as if the Aces or Tide would somehow catch them at any moment. He handed her his phone. "Call my mom," he said, to give her something to do. His mom had probably already heard from one of her sons or husband.

In halting, clipped syllables, Shannon relayed some of the details. "And he, Viper, I mean, he tried to cut out the car seat…" She stopped and gulped for air. He took the phone from her cold fingers.

"We'll be there in a couple, Mama," he said and disconnected.

They were home in a short while, his mother listening, wide-eyed, to the rest of the details, with Annabell tucked safely in her embrace.

"Do you think Viper will ever figure out he tried to steal a car seat with a five-pound sack of flour aboard?" Keegan said, laughing.

When the baby fussed, Jack was surprised to see Shannon hold out her arms. Evie reluctantly gave her the baby, and she walked to the guest room. He left his family to wait for the police and followed. He heard sniffles.

"Shan?" he said from the doorway.

She turned to hide the tears, but not fast enough.

"Hey." He went to her, touching her arm. "You okay?"

"I don't know why I'm crying," she said with a touch of anger, as if daring him to come up with a reason.

"Well, now, the shooting and all. That was upsetting."

"It's not that."

"What, then?"

She bit her lip, and he gave her time.

"When Viper tried to take the car seat, she could have been in there." Her lip trembled. "Her tiny head. A baby's skull is in pieces, really," she said, as if presenting in a classroom, only there was a manic quality to it. "The little pieces are held together by cranial sutures. The fontanels. Completely unable to withstand any trauma. Think what could have happened. Just think."

He stared at her, openmouthed. "But she wasn't anywhere near, Shan. We never would have put her life at risk."

"I know. I know," she wailed suddenly, "but imagining his filthy hands on her, I just… I can't stop thinking about what if it had been her in that car seat." A choking sob cut off her words. "There's something wrong with me," she cried. "I'm a doctor. I'm used to drama. And I don't like babies. Not really." Tears ran unchecked, dripping from her chin and onto Annabell's head.

He turned her very gently in the circle of his arms and held them both to his chest, pressing a kiss to the top of her head. "Honeybunch, there's nothing wrong with you. Nothing at all."

He let her cry, catching her tears on his shirt-front, left in wonderment at the complexity of a woman's heart.

Shannon tapped her foot as Larraby listened to their report with Keegan, Barrett and Tom adding details into the conversation.

"The situation has changed," Larraby said. "I'm bringing in cops from the county because the Aces are all over Gold Bar, searching for Tides. And when they aren't searching, they're tearing things up. I've had four drunk and dis-orderlies already this morning." He looked at Jack and Shannon. "How'd they get Dina's cell phone?"

"I don't know," Shannon said. "I've been try-ing to figure that out myself."

"This is getting complicated." Jack related the conversation with Tiffany. "It's possible Pinball wants to make a covert deal to get Dina and the baby and hand them over to the Tide to prevent a conflict or hide them until the Tides give up."

"That strategy isn't exactly working so far," Larraby said.

"Or are some of his people going behind Pinball's back?" Shannon asked.

Jack shook his head. "I don't know."

"I…" Her phone rang with an unknown number. "Should I?"

Larraby nodded.

She answered.

"It's me."

Shannon was so elated to hear Dina's voice, she almost dropped the phone. She hit the speaker button. "Dina, where have you been?"

"Looking for my brother, like I said." Dina sounded stressed, tired. "I arranged a meeting with him. Tomorrow."

"Who is your brother that you have to arrange meetings?" Jack snapped. "What is he, a senator or something?"

"He's a powerful guy."

"The law-abiding kind?" Jack said.

There was a long pause. "He's gonna help me, once I talk to him face-to-face. That's all that matters. How is Annabell?"

Shannon explained the ambush at the airstrip. Dina's voice dropped nearly to a whisper.

"Someone stole my backpack from the gas-station bathroom. I think they've been following me. They must have used my phone to set up the airstrip ambush."

"Who? Someone with the Tide?"

"I don't know."

Barrett and Keegan exchanged a worried look.

"Dina," Shannon said. "This isn't safe. They're after you, and they're close. You need to meet us, and we have to go to the cops."

"Uh-uh."

"There's a cop in town. His name is Larraby, and he's okay. He can help you."

"No," Dina said loudly. "No cops. Tomorrow. Just keep her until tomorrow. I will call you by midnight. I promise. Please." Her voice broke. "I can't stand to be away from her, but I have to do this, or we'll never have the kind of life she deserves."

"Dina," Shannon started, tone gentler. "Please listen to reason. Your baby is in danger, and so are you."

"Tomorrow," Dina said. "Midnight." And then she disconnected.

Larraby huffed out a breath. "I should call social services."

"What's one more day?" Jack said.

"Something is going on with Dina that she isn't coming clean about," Tom said. "Why won't

she tell you who her brother is? Who's been following her? For what purpose?"

Shannon rubbed her temples where an ache
had begun to pound.

There was a knock at the door, and Evie led
a man into the room. Shannon shot to her feet.

"Hello," he said with a pleasant smile. "I'm
Detective Mason from the LAPD. It's taken me
a while to track you down, Dr. Livingston." He
waved a hand. "My apologies. I mean Dr. Thorn.
We have some things to discuss."

"I… I'm sorry, but I'm very tired," she managed. "Can we talk later?"

His mouth tightened. "No," he said. "We need
to talk now. Right now."

ELEVEN

"I didn't know you were in town." Jack didn't miss the muscle twitching in Larraby's jaw. "Why didn't you call?" Larraby said.

"Because you're lousy at returning your messages." Mason's lips thinned into a hard line. "I've left a half dozen."

Larraby flushed. "Busy here."

"And I'm busy there. You're not the only county with gang troubles. We got a few in LA, in case you don't read the newspaper." Mason turned his back on Larraby.

Jack moved closer to Shannon, resting his arm on the sofa and gathering her hand in his. Her skin was cold. "What do you want, Detective?"

"I want to straighten out a little matter of Dina Brown's baby. I've done some inquiries." He stared at Shannon. "You didn't give birth, Dr. Livingston, at least nowhere in the state of California that I can find."

Shannon clutched his hand.

Jack fixed the guy with a hard stare. "You within your rights to be investigating my wife?"

Mason didn't spare a glance at Jack, skewering Shannon in his sights. "The baby you're caring for, it's Dina Brown's, isn't it?"

Shannon gulped. "She…she asked us to watch her for a few days, and that's what we're doing."

"She's a criminal."

"She hasn't been charged with anything," Larraby said. "No laws broken in asking a friend to watch your baby."

"The thing is," Mason said, "T.J. has taken a turn for the worse, you see. He's not expected to live, but he woke up just long enough to tell me that Dina pushed him down the stairs."

"That was convenient," Jack said. "Him saying that just when you were visiting."

Mason glared. "I'll ignore that implication. It's enough for you to know that if he dies, it will become a murder investigation, and Dina Brown will be the prime suspect."

"The doctor in charge is giving him a fifty-percent chance," Shannon said. "I checked this morning. Funny, he didn't mention that you had been there with T.J."

"The point is," Mason said, "he's not likely to make it, and the best thing for the baby will be to hand her over to social services. She'll be well taken care of."

Larraby jerked his chin at Mason. "And you came here, all this way, because you want the best for Dina's baby?"

"No," Mason said. "I'm here to make my job easier. The Tide is going to come gunning for Dina with both barrels if T.J. dies. They'll rip this town apart to get to anyone helping her, and that's going to mean an all-out war with the Aces. I'm doing my job as a police officer to keep the peace here. You should be doing the same."

"I am," Larraby snapped. "We're putting every possible resource into keeping the lid on things."

"No, you're not." Mason waited a beat. "You're keeping an infant at risk by hiding her here. Well, the lid's off now, Larraby. Both the Aces and the Tides are in town. Tides aren't leaving until they get Dina or the baby. Aces aren't leaving until they drive out the Tide. Only way to keep the peace is to arrest Dina. If we take the baby, she'll turn herself in."

"You don't know that."

"Well, let's just say she won't have much reason to stay in the area, and neither will the bikers."

Shannon locked her eyes on Mason, something ferocious in her expression. "I saw you take an envelope from Cruiser at the hospital the day T.J. was brought in. You're on the Tide's payroll. That's why you want the baby. You're tracking her down to hand her over to them, not the cops or social services."

Mason concealed his shock quickly. "You're mistaken, Doctor. You should be careful about making accusations."

"And you should be going now," Jack said, standing. "I don't like the way you're talking to my wife."

Barrett, Tom and Keegan stood also, lending silent support.

Mason swept cold eyes across the whole room. "You're playing a dangerous game with a baby's life. I hope you can live with yourselves when it falls apart and someone dies." He strode to the door, tossing one more comment over his shoulder.

"You know, Dr. Livingston, reputation is everything, isn't it? How's it gonna look when the hospital board finds out their new doctor has been lying about having a baby, covering for a gang member?"

"Dina's not a gang member," Shannon snapped.

"Dina belongs to the Tide," Mason said. "And she'll never escape that."

"Get out," Jack said. "Now."

Mason left.

For a moment, no one said anything. Larraby

got to his feet. "He's right about one thing. The safest choice left to us is to put Annabell into the care of social services or protective custody. Dina may or may not escape a criminal charge, but at least her kid will be safe."

"One more day," Shannon said. "That's all Dina needs—one more day." She held herself around the middle. "If she doesn't call by midnight tomorrow, you can do what you think is best."

"All right." Larraby turned to go.

"But not Mason," Jack said. "If it comes to that, can you arrange for them to take custody without going through Mason?"

"I think I can make that happen." Larraby crammed his hat on his head and shoved wearily out the door.

Shannon sank onto the sofa with a groan. "He's right about reputation. I may not have an internship left to finish by the time this is over."

Jack took a breath and knelt next to her. His family melted away into the kitchen, talking quietly. "Shan…" He waited until her frightened eyes found his. "If you need to go back, do it."

She started. "What do you mean?"

"I know how important your work is to you." He took another fortifying gulp of oxygen. "If you need to go back to Los Angeles, I'll support that. I'll fly you there, even."

"But Annabell…"

"I'll take care of Annabell and handle whatever comes."

She cocked her head, lips parted, soft as velvet. "You would do that?"

I would do anything, his heart said. "Yes," he said simply.

"But all these years, you've tried to persuade me to come back, to stay here, and now you're clearing the way for me to go? Why?"

"I wanted you to be happy with me, Shan, but I understand that's not going to happen, so I'll have to settle for you being happy without me." He forced a smile. "Dumb old cowboy, offering to fly his wife out of his life, huh?"

Her expression was caught between wonder and disbelief. Finally, she jerked away and stood. "If you think I'm going to let Mason intimidate me, then you don't know me very well, Jack Thorn. I will decide when I need to return to LA, and you can be sure it won't be a moment before I'm good and ready. You got me, Cowboy?"

He climbed to his feet. "Yes, ma'am."

"Fine, then." She whirled on her heel and marched off to the kitchen.

Keegan lounged in the doorway, smiling broadly. "Saddle up, Jack," he said. "Looks like things are gonna get bumpier from here on in."

As if that's possible.

* * *

Shannon continued to keep tabs on T.J.'s condition, which was as dire as Mason had suggested, thanks to a rising infection. If he died, the legal pressure would hitch up to a whole new level for Dina. And the baby.

Shannon did not understand her own burgeoning feelings for Annabell. Babies were enormous, lifelong commitments. And the potential to make colossal mistakes in their upbringing was bone-chilling, yet she found herself constantly worrying about Annabell. And also enjoying every fascinating moment. What was it about the scent of her sweet skin that made her pick her up just to experience it? She could understand why Dina would go to such risks to secure a future for her daughter, and she knew her own mother would do the same for her. The power of the parent bond was heady stuff. Though she hadn't had much of a bond with her father, maybe one was more than enough of a blessing.

Her thoughts returned to Dina. Something from their hurried conversation about her brother would not fade from her mind. While Shelby and Evie were giving Annabell a bath, she opened up her laptop and began to dig in.

Jack arrived in the kitchen at lunchtime, sweaty and moving gingerly as he washed his hands. "Had to load a reluctant horse into the trailer for his owner. Harder than getting Keegan to the dentist. What are you working on?"

"Dina Brown," she said as her fingers tapped across the keys. "I thought if we figured out what she was hiding, it could help."

He drained a glass of water and sat down next to her. "Got anything?"

"I was just looking at my notes in her medical file. I had forgotten she'd been a patient of mine a couple of years ago in the emergency room. When she first came in, I treated her for a sprained wrist and a cracked rib. She made up some story about falling, of course, and would not admit to abuse. She had no cell phone, and I remembered I asked if there was anyone I could call for her. She gave me a cell-phone number, and I called it via the hospital phone. There was no answer. I only remember because it upset her."

"You didn't happen to write down that number, did you?"

"No, but I know the date and time I made the call per my notes, and I can ask my computer-whiz friend at the hospital to look it up for me on the outgoing call log."

He whistled. "Might be nothing, but then again, might not."

She messaged her friend, and in an hour, she had the cell-phone number Dina had called.

"Can Larraby trace it?" she said.

"We'll find out soon. I just texted him the number."

Shelby and Evie carried Annabell in. She was dressed in a fresh pink onesie with matching socks, and inexplicably, Shannon's heart lurched. Jack intercepted and snagged the baby.

"Little Bit, you look like a million bucks and change." He beamed, positively radiating happiness as he paraded her around the room before settling her in a bouncy seat. Barrett, Tom and Keegan joined them, and Shelby and Evie doled out rich tomato soup and grilled cheese sandwiches. Barrett could not stop staring at his wife. He raised his water glass and cleared his throat.

"I would like to propose a toast to Shelby, my wife..." He paused. "...and the mother of my child."

The room went dead quiet for a moment. Evie's mouth was open in a wide O-shape of astonishment. "You mean you're...expecting?"

Shelby nodded, eyes wet. "Looks like the family tree will have another Thorn next spring."

Tom let out a whoop of joy, and Evie burst into happy tears. Keegan and Jack kissed Shelby and pounded Barrett on the back.

"'Bout time someone started the next generation," Jack said.

Keegan grinned. "I'm gonna teach Barrett Jr. all my best tricks."

"No, you won't," Barrett said firmly.

There was laughter around the table, and Shannon added her own hugs and congratulations. She caught the look in Jack's eyes. Joy, yes, but shot through with something else. He turned the blue gaze on her, and she read the question there.

Why not us, Shan?

Why not? Because…there were so many reasons she could not begin to count.

If you need to go back to Los Angeles, I'll support that. I'll fly you there, even. It was cruel for her to stay and make him think that their future might be possible. And the real truth of it was she knew she would not make Jack happy. He deserved a woman who would put him first.

Purposefully, she turned away and tuned back in to the bubbling conversation about plans to finish the house, furnish a nursery and all the happy speculation swirling around the promise of new life. It really was something to marvel at, she thought.

A marvel for someone else. She had an internship to return to, far away from the sleepy town of Gold Bar and Jack, a town that would stifle her and a man who deserved so much better.

Jack stayed close to home to handle the chores and watch over Shannon and Annabell, who had spent a quiet morning together. His brother's news had hit him with a broadside slap as he made his way to the stables. Barrett deserved happiness more than anyone after losing his first wife to a drunk driver, and Owen had found his perfect match, as well, in Ella Cahill. What was it about Jack that made him want a woman who didn't want him? Having Shannon on the ranch was exquisite torture, ripping away all his brave notions that he'd gotten over her. She'd made it clear as glass that she did not want a life with him any more than she had seven years before. So why, oh, why could he not simply accept it and start over? His brain screamed at him to do so, but he could not shake the feeling that deep down, under the carefully constructed mask, Shannon felt something for him. His pride talking?

Breathing in the scent of the clean straw he'd just laid down in the stable, he set to work grooming Lady. Starting in with the currycomb, he loosened the dirt in her coat, feeling her long lean lines. The circular sweeps over her hips left her relaxed, and they'd grown to trust each other enough that she'd overcome her sensitivity about having her belly and back legs brushed. Still, he kept the pressure soft and easy. He combed out the tangles in her mane and tail. Then he employed the body brush to whisk away the dirt he'd loosened with the currycomb. A wipe of the eyes and ears with a soft cloth, and a kiss to her muzzle, finished things off. He watched her meander out to the pasture and took pleasure in it as he did every day. There was no finer view than Lady cropping brilliant green grass against an azure sky.

He recalled his promise to Shannon that he would live where she chose in order to keep their marriage alive. Could he actually leave Gold Bar? Pull up stakes and relocate to Southern California or New York or any of the places Shannon talked about setting up practice? There was only one woman, one heart that could pry him from this ground. Could he do it? He could, but only for her.

Only for Shannon.

He was surprised to see Shannon standing along the fence with Annabell in her arms.

"Do you see the horses, Annabell? Uncle Jack is taking care of them." The baby wore a little sun hat and the tiniest pair of socks he'd ever seen. She was carefully cuddled in a blanket to keep off the breeze.

"I'm Uncle Jack now? Sounds like I belong in a nursery rhyme."

"Yes, and I'm Auntie Shannon, so don't complain."

"Wasn't," he said with a smile. "Took her bottle okay?"

"Like a champ. We did some tummy time to develop arm strength, and we read a couple of picture books. Well, I read, and she listened and drooled, mostly."

He laughed. "Shannon, you're the best at this."

Her shoulders tensed.

"What? Did I say something wrong?"

She fussed with Annabell's hat. "No. Nothing."

He tugged playfully at the back of her shirt. "Not nothing. Uncle Jack should know when he's messed up."

She pressed a cheek to the baby's head and let out a breath. "My dad used to say that. When I brought home a perfect test, I was the best, and he would smile and brag on me to anyone who would listen. One question wrong, though—" she shrugged "—then there was no smile." She sighed. "Jack, your parents told you to do your best. My dad said, 'Be the best, or don't bother showing up.'"

"That's a lot of pressure on a kid."

"I learned that lesson early on. Being the best

got my dad's attention because it helped him feel good about himself to brag about me. Nothing else I did warranted a second look."

Jack rapped a fist against the fence. "It's wrong, Shan. Love isn't like that. It's not a brass scale like the one at the inn, love on one side, achievements on the other."

"It is for my father."

"But not your mom."

"No, she didn't ever expect me to be perfect, but I am all she has, and that's a heavy weight sometimes, too. She'd never say it, but the thought of her daughter being an accomplished doctor feels like the one thing she can be proud of in this life."

"So you gotta be the best for the father who left you and the mother who didn't. That's crazy."

"We can't all have perfect families like you did," she snapped.

"I'm blessed, I know, but what your father did to you was wrong."

She let out a long, low breath. "It's hard to never be enough, but it made me strong."

He could not stop himself from trailing a finger along her forearm. "You are enough, Shannon. You're enough."

She turned a tortured look at him, and it burned inside that he could not erase what her father had done. "Enough for whom?" she said softly.

"For me, and for God."

Her eyes went dark. "I… I don't feel like enough. Maybe I never will."

He kept his hand on her arm. "Look at Annabell, Shan. Look at her." For a moment, they gazed at the perfect child in Shannon's embrace. "If she doesn't become a doctor or a rocket scientist or get straight As in school, should Dina withhold love? Treat her like she's a failure?"

Shannon did not answer. He realized she was crying, and he wrapped her and Annabell in an embrace. "You're enough, honey," he whispered. "More than enough."

She pulled away when his family turned into the drive, his parents' SUV with Barrett and Shelby in the back, probably discussing plans about the new addition to the family. Keegan jogged into the house, hungry as always, Jack thought, though he'd probably eaten a plateful of snacks after the service.

Shannon dashed her tears away with a quick move and separated herself from him. "Tonight," she said. "Tonight, Dina will call."

"Any word from Larraby on that cell-phone number?"

"Not yet."

His mother waved to them and called out. "Come on in the house."

Barrett held the car door for Shelby, and she climbed out.

A buzzing vibration filled the air and shot through his muscles. As soon as his brain deciphered the sound, he started shoving Shannon toward the house.

"Get inside," he shouted.

"Jack…" she gasped, but he continued to both propel and support her, desperate to see her through the front door.

"Barrett," he hollered.

Barrett had seen them, too, and before they could formulate any kind of a plan, the long drive was filled with a dozen bikers sporting Tide colors.

The bikers began firing their weapons, bullets peppering the porch and shattering the front windows. Jack pushed her behind the SUV, and Barrett did the same with Shelby. Tom shoved Evie there a moment later.

With bullets flying, they could not risk the dash to the house. The rear-window glass shattered next, sending fragments showering down on them. Shannon arced her torso over the baby to protect her. The shrill whinny of frightened horses carried over the whoops of the Tide as they closed in.

Jack pressed a phone into Shelby's hand. "Call the cops."

Shelby attempted to do so with shaking hands as Barrett crouched over her. Jack looked around desperately. He'd have to draw their fire. Create a distraction long enough for his family to get into the house. Shannon grabbed his wrist.

"Don't you even think about it," she said.

He started to answer when a volley of shots came from the other direction.

Keegan was behind the porch pillars, laying down cover fire for all he was worth.

Jack and Barrett didn't waste a moment, knowing a moment might be all they had.

Shannon gasped as Jack pulled her to her feet.

"Run. Now," he commanded.

In a haze of terror, she sprinted toward the house, following Barrett, who was between Shelby and the bikers. Revving engines and shouts and the din of bullets nearly robbed her of her senses, but somehow, she clung to the baby and ran.

Shelby and Barrett barreled through first. She stumbled in behind them. Shannon wanted to stop and find Jack, but Barrett wouldn't allow it, propelling them both to the stairwell at the back of the kitchen.

"Basement. Stay there until it's over."

"Barrett," Shelby called, terror on her face,

but he was already turning away. Shelby swallowed and took Shannon's elbow. "This is one time we'd better follow orders."

Shannon trailed Shelby down a steep staircase, into a large carpeted room with an old rocking chair. The space was cool, slightly musty, the tall shelves crowded with old harnesses and saddles and boxes of jars waiting for their supply of tomatoes from Evie's garden.

With Shelby's help, she laid Annabell onto the floor. She immediately unwrapped the sobbing baby and checked her tiny limbs for injuries. Shannon's fingers trembled, but she talked as soothingly as she could. The little body was uninjured, whole and healthy.

She expelled a breath that came all the way from the depths of her soul. "Thank You, God," she said, surprised that the utterance felt like the most natural thing in the world.

"I'll second that," Shelby added.

Shannon rewrapped the baby and started pacing in tight circles and patting Annabell's back. Could the Thorns defend their ranch until the police arrived? Another round of shots made her cry out.

"Sounds closer," Shelby said, eyes wide.

Shannon's nerves iced over as someone climbed down the stairs. She and Shelby shrank back into the dark corner, waiting with breath held until Evie came into view.

She ran to them. "Are you hurt? The baby?"

"No," Shelby assured her. "We're okay. Annabell is, too. You? The…the men?"

Her mouth contorted. "Barrett, Tom and Jack got their rifles, and they're giving those bikers the what for until the cops arrive."

"But they're outnumbered," Shannon said. "How can they…?"

Her eyes sparked. "Shannon, any one of my boys can shoot the wings off a fly. They're in the house, protected, and the cops are on their way, so don't let your nerves get the better of you."

After a countering flare of anger, Shannon realized that Evie, too, needed to believe her own words. Her precious boys and her husband were in a standoff with criminals who would not hesitate to mow them down. Worse, Shannon had brought that trouble here, delivered it squarely into the Thorns' home and given it a seat at the table.

Evie held out her arms to take Annabell. Though Shannon desperately craved the comfort of holding Annabell, she recognized the need in Evie's face, the shadow of fear under the strong lines. Evie Thorn was terrified, too, though she would not ever give voice to the feelings. Wordlessly, she handed over the baby, and just as silently, Evie thanked her for the gesture. Something passed between them in that moment, and Shannon was struck again by the yawning depth of a parent's love for her child. There was something otherworldly about that connection, something most definitely divine, deeper than genes, infinitely stronger than science.

A thunk against the basement wall made them jump. Again, the door opened, and a set of boots clomped down the stairs.

Viper? Cruiser? Shannon felt a scream bubble up in her throat until she realized it was a pair of well-worn cowboy boots headed down the stairs, an old pair that had been resoled many times.

Jack hit the bottom, his gaze frantic. Barrett was right behind him. "Is anyone…?"

"No," Shannon said. "None of us are injured."

Sweat stood out on his brow, and his shirt was torn at the shoulder. Barrett scooped his mother, Annabell and his wife in a two-armed hug. "Cops are here. Bikers turned tail and ran. Dad and Keegan are checking the horses."

Shannon's limbs felt as if they moved automatically as she threw herself against Jack's chest. She had not realized she was trembling all over until he stroked his palms up and down her shoulders.

"It's okay," he murmured into her hair, but she could not stop the shaking. He dipped his chin, his lips skimming her ear. "Good guys won."

"Let's go upstairs to the kitchen," Evie said as she passed them. "I'll put on some coffee."

"Mom's answer to everything is found in the kitchen," Jack whispered, his warm breath still tingling her senses.

"I heard that, Jack," Evie said, giving him a poke in the back on her way up the stairs.

With effort, Shannon detached herself, though Jack kept a hold on her elbow and tethered her to him.

She wanted to do all kinds of nutty things, such as smooth his hair, press her palm to his cheek and feel the vibrant warmth there, to simply stare at the exquisitely blue eyes. Giving herself a mental shake, she cleared her throat. "I'm okay."

"Sure?"

She straightened. "Yes, sure. I was just shaky there for a minute. A bit of psychogenic shock. Sudden dilation of blood vessels. I'm fine now."

He shot her that crooked grin. "Whatever you say, Doc."

She forced her limbs to stop quivering and her body to stop craving Jack's embrace and climbed the stairs, hoping he didn't notice how she had to clutch the railing.

It was a normal reaction to an abnormal, shocking situation to throw herself into Jack's arms like that. Perfectly normal. She tried to tell herself.

Whatever you say, Doc.

TWELVE

His mom was already brewing coffee, and Annabell was in her bouncy seat, gumming a fist. Larraby roamed outside, taking pictures, while they waited in the kitchen.

Barrett paced, and Jack waited patiently for whatever was coming. He knew his brother, a big bear of a man who thought long and talked short, had something to say.

"Horses are okay. Spooked, mostly, but they'll recover," Keegan said, also eyeing his eldest brother as he helped himself to two oatmeal raisin cookies from the jar.

Barrett completed another circle around the linoleum, stopped and faced the table. "I'm sorry. I feel bad saying it, but this can't continue."

"What do you mean?" Evie said. Tom edged behind her, his fingers caressing his wife's neck.

Barrett scrubbed a hand over his beard. "The baby, Shannon, here at the ranch."

Jack's jaw went tight. "You're not saying we should kick them out."

"I don't want that, of course. I want them safe, but not here."

Jack stood now, meeting his brother's hard stare. "They're in danger everywhere else."

"They're in danger here," Barrett snapped, "and I can't allow that to bleed over and expose our family, too." His gaze traveled to Shelby. "My wife, our baby. I can't risk their safety. I'm sorry."

Jack felt fiery heat rise to his face. Barrett's wife, Barrett's baby. Well, maybe Jack's own marriage was a farce, but he burned to defend and protect it. Toss Shannon and Annabell out? No way. No how. He faced his brother, and it was like looking at a bigger, broader version of himself. "To keep your wife safe, you'd toss mine out?"

"Don't make it like that, Jack."

"I'm not. You are." Adrenaline pumped hot through his veins. It would have been a relief if Barrett threw a punch, if their anger and fear tumbled out in a wrestling match or a fight, anything to release that unbearable tension.

Barrett's hands hung loose at his sides. "Jack," he said.

One syllable from his brother, and the agony it contained was a reminder to Jack. Barrett had lost a wife, a woman they'd all loved and adored. His big brother had been stripped of his soul mate in one horrific moment that almost ended Barrett's will to live, too. Those had been dark times, terrible years that they'd only survived thanks to the grace of God. Jack stemmed the hard words that were about to spill from his mouth. Heaving out a breath, he took a step back. "I get it, Barrett, but I'm going to protect them," he said simply. "I'll figure out another way."

A shimmer of relief shone in his brother's gaze. "They need to go into police custody. The cops can keep them safe until Dina shows or doesn't." His shoulders drooped. "I'm sorry. I don't want to say this, but I can't look myself in the mirror knowing my family is a target. I…"

Shannon rose and put a hand on Barrett's. "You're right, Barrett. No need to apologize for having the courage to say it."

Jack's throat thickened as he heard the understanding embedded in her tone.

She let out a breath. "I'll take Annabell and go back to the inn until midnight. If we don't hear from Dina, I'll hand the baby over to Larraby."

"We," Jack said, through the stab of pain in his gut. "We will stay together, and not at the inn. They'll be watching there. I'll take you somewhere else, a place nobody knows about. Somewhere we'll have the upper hand."

Tom raised an eyebrow. "The fishing lodge?"

"Yeah. I'll take them up in the SUV. It will be bumpy."

Shannon smiled. "At this point, what's a few more bumps?"

Evie poured her more coffee. "It's a two-bedroom, but it's rustic. Tom built it early on in our marriage, when we had this notion that roughing it was some sort of noble idea."

Tom kissed her temple. "Come on. You loved those days fishing and living off the land."

She laughed. "I didn't love the snakes."

Shannon blanched. "I could have done without knowing there are snakes."

"Not many in the spring," Jack said. "We won't be hiking around their territory, anyway. Strictly a shelter in place until tomorrow."

"I'll go, too, on horseback," Keegan said. "I'll bring up Prince for some added insurance, in case you need to escape onto the mountain. Motorcycles can't follow you there." He caught Shannon's eye and winked. "Don't worry. Those bikers would be too scared by the snakes to stick around, even if they did know where the lodge was located."

Shannon gave him a sassy toss of the head.

Shelby sighed. "I wish I could go and help you but…"

"But you won't," Barrett said.

"I know, but still. It's not going to be easy with a baby if this place is as rustic as you say."

"Keeg and I can help," Jack said.

Annabell let out a cry, and Keegan tensed. "Uh, I'm just there for equestrian support. I don't do babies, only if they have four legs and a whinny."

Jack shook his head. "Pathetic."

"I'll go," Evie said. Tom frowned, but she waved him off with a dish towel. "She can't tend a baby by herself in that place."

"Yes, I can," Shannon said.

"Know how to operate a woodstove?" Evie said.

Shannon deflated. "Uh, no."

"That's what I thought. I'll put some food together, and we'll go. Tom, Barrett and Shelby can keep the ranch going for one day without me. Right?"

"We'll try," Shelby said. "No promises."

Shannon shook her head. "I appreciate it, I really do, but Barrett is right. I don't want Evie and Keegan to put themselves at risk." She shot a look at Jack. "Can't you tell them?"

Jack shrugged. "I can tell them, but I've seen

that look on their faces before. The only person in this family more stubborn than Keegan is Mama."

"I can attest to that," Tom said. His soft gaze found Shannon. "You're family, Shannon. You always have been, no matter what your legal status is or isn't. We don't turn our backs on family."

Shannon stood rigid and stiff, and Jack wanted to reach out to her, but more than that, he wanted her to accept his father's words. The Thorns did not turn their back on family, but her own father had, and it left such a wide rip that only God could heal it.

Her pain ran deep, but he hoped there would eventually be a place where she could allow God to mend the torn edges of her soul.

"Thank you. I… That is so kind, especially in light of all the pain I've caused."

Tom smiled. "I've got to see about boarding up the broken windows and ordering some new glass."

"I'll help clean up," Barrett said, avoiding Jack's eyes, "and get some rifles cleaned and loaded for you to take to the lodge."

As he passed, Jack stopped him. "Would have said the same thing in your place."

Barrett clasped Jack's shoulder in a fierce grip that said everything without a single word.

* * *

Jack and Shannon climbed into the front seat that afternoon, after Evie commandeered the back in order to sit next to Annabell. Shannon kept her phone close, but there was still no word from Dina or from Larraby about the cell number she'd called from the hospital in Los Angeles. The only text was from her supervising doctor.

Do you intend to return and finish your internship or not?

Panic seized her. *Yes, yes, yes*, she wanted to shout, though she tried to keep her tone professional as she mentally composed a reply. Every day that passed of her unscheduled leave would no doubt reinforce to the hospital board that she was throwing away her excruciatingly hard-earned opportunity. How many more days before they told her not to bother coming back?

What was she doing here in Gold Bar? Spinning her wheels, risking her life, developing feelings she didn't want for a family and a man she'd walked away from.

"Something wrong?" Jack said.

What isn't? she wanted to say. Instead, she shook her head and stared out the window.

The road up the mountain to the lodge was

bordered with a thick fringe of trees and shrubbery, the mountain quilted in every conceivable shade of green. A perfect day for a drive, yet her stomach remained clenched in a tight knot. After an hour and a half of steady uphill, Jack turned off the main road and tackled a gravel path that gave them all a good shaking.

"Keegan's just texted me he's arrived," Evie said.

"Faster by horseback, but there's the baby-seat problem," Jack joked.

Shannon could not make herself smile, so she settled on a nod.

"Gonna be over soon," Jack said, fingers skimming hers.

And that was part of the problem, she thought. Spending such intimate time with Jack and the Thorns would make it harder to do what she knew must be done: their divorce. It was unfair, how she'd handled things, running away, keeping Jack close with a marriage license, when she knew he deserved to live his own life and find someone else. And then dragging him back into her orbit with a desperate plea she knew he would not turn away from.

Over soon. Jack was right. Once Annabell was safe with her mother, Shannon would return to her emergency room and dissolve her marriage. Pain lanced her heart. Shoving away the cascade of emotion, she sat up straighter as the lodge came into view. It was a rectangular one-story building, wood sided and hemmed in by trees on every side. Claustrophobic, Shannon thought. Around the back of the house was a fenced area and a horse shelter. Inside were two horses, including Jack's Lady, exploring their temporary digs.

At Jack's instruction, Evie extricated the baby and left the car seat fastened in. Shannon grabbed the diaper bag, and Jack gathered up some bulging paper grocery sacks in one arm and a small generator in the other.

She raised an eyebrow. "No electricity?"

"No, ma'am. This will make sure we can keep our phones charged."

He'd thought of everything, but then, Jack was a planner by nature. How she'd thrown his life into disarray when she'd called him after fleeing Los Angeles, she didn't want to consider.

They entered the dark interior. It was musty and cool. Shannon wanted to turn around and go back to the SUV, but she swallowed and followed Evie to a bedroom, where someone, Keegan likely, had set up a portable crib. There were two small beds and a minuscule bathroom with a skylight that let in the sun. Evie flashed a smile. "See? Not so bad. No rodents or snakes, and there's indoor plumbing. I insisted on that."

Shannon went to the window. A great wall of

mountain rose up behind the property, and she saw an eagle soaring slowly above. A slice of creek was visible, fringed by cattails, with water bugs darting along the surface of the water. It was lovely, quiet and so very isolated.

If they were found here by Cruiser…

She jumped as Evie touched her back. "I'm going to go work on some minestrone for dinner. Takes a long time to get water boiling up here, so I need a good head start. Call me if you need help with the baby."

"I will."

Evie walked to the door.

"Mrs. Thorn…"

"Evie," she said.

"Evie…thank you. I mean, for everything."

Evie nodded. "You're welcome, Shannon." She stopped with one foot out the door. "Oh, by the way. That blue bag is for you. It was delivered to the house yesterday, and Jack said to make sure to bring it along."

"Okay." After Evie left, she opened the bag and took out a foil-wrapped box. Chocolates. They were from Val's shop, she realized, the woman who had rescued Jack at the clinic. Chocolates. Amid that whole drama, he'd bought her candy. The box indicated they were truffles, hand-dipped in both milk and dark chocolate, her undisputed favorites. Underneath the box was a fuzzy bunny toy, plump and soft, with a little rattle inside that sounded like rain. A toy for Annabell, their pretend child.

She sat on the cot, staring at the box of chocolates and squeezing the bunny to her cheek, emotions tumbling in ways she did not understand.

"You found them?"

She jerked. Jack stood at the door, holding a pair of leather work gloves, every inch the tall, strong, blue-eyed cowboy. For a moment, she forgot everything she'd meant to say to him as a sudden yearning to embrace him flooded over her.

"Uh, yes. Thank you," she managed, "but you shouldn't have bought chocolates for me."

He shrugged. "I remembered how much you liked them from our dating days, the kind with squishy stuff in the middle, right? I figured you could use a treat."

Our dating days... "Jack," she said. "Please. Please don't misunderstand. You can't treat me like we're dating or married or anything. I'm leaving." Her heart twisted desperately. "I'm leaving just as soon as I can. We are going to make it official this time, the divorce." Her stomach felt suddenly ripped in two, but she kept her expression steady.

He went still. "I know."

"I don't want you to think that there's something between us again."

"I don't."

She waved the box. "This is…"

"Candy, that's all." His voice held an edge. "If you don't want it, toss it."

"I'm sorry," she said. "It was sweet of you, but…"

"But you don't want sweet," he snapped. "You don't want Gold Bar, and you don't want me." He jammed the gloves in his back pocket. "Don't worry. I got it. Forget about the chocolates. Sorry they upset you. Dumb idea."

As he whirled on his boot and stalked away, her mind and heart warred with each other. She knew what she wanted, and she'd said as much to anyone who would listen. Why, then, did she ache for Jack Thorn?

Do it before you lose your nerve.

Yanking out her phone, she was relieved to find that she had service. Quickly, she called and left a voice-mail message for her supervising doctor.

I will be back in Los Angeles by Wednesday evening, at the latest.

The gold band on her finger drew her attention.

She was one step further on the road to her heart's desire, the emergency room, her internship, everything she wished for. So why did she have a feeling it would be the end of the world to take that ring off her finger for good?

THIRTEEN

Jack could not extinguish the anger that rippled through him. It took a few hours of tending the horses, another hour of riding to check out the area, oiling his rifle and unpacking their scant supplies before he realized he was entirely to blame for his sorry state. As dusk crept over the tall grass, he slammed the ax into the sturdy log, his own actions rising up to convict him. Shannon was not interested in making their marriage work, so why in the world had he allowed his feelings for her to flame to life like dry tinder? A deluded sap, that was what he was, buying her chocolates. What had possessed him?

Get yourself together, he thought, ripping the ax through a log and hauling the pieces inside. He stacked them on the stone hearth and washed up before settling himself at the kitchen table, where his mother ladled out bowls of soup. It was a cool evening, the gathering darkness arriving quickly as the lodge fell into the shadow of the mountain.

Shannon settled Annabell onto a blanket and joined them at the table. She made no effort to generate conversation until Evie pressed.

"I apologize for overhearing your phone call," she said. "But we're in pretty close quarters here. You were making plans to return to the emergency room?"

Shannon nodded. "Yes. I told them I'd be back Wednesday night, at the latest."

Wednesday. Good to know the exact date their marriage would be over, so their divorce proceedings could begin. On Wednesday, he would restart Jack Thorn's life, part two. The part without her.

"I... I imagined everything would be settled by then," Shannon said.

He felt her gaze on him, but he kept his eyes on his soup and offered a casual shrug. "Sure. The baby issue will be squared away. Nothing keeping you here."

Keegan and his mother exchanged a look, which he pretended not to notice. The rest of the meal passed in awkward spurts of forced conversation, until, mercifully, it was done.

"I'll help you with the dishes, Mama," Keegan offered, gathering up plates and disappearing into the kitchen, with his mother right behind.

Shannon settled into the rocking chair and offered Annabell the bottle Evie had prepared. Soon they would both be gone from his life.

Nothing keeping you here. He gulped some water to ease his suddenly dry throat.

"I'm sorry," Shannon said, startling him.

"About what?"

"That I didn't pursue a divorce earlier."

His gut pinched. "Got another guy waiting to marry you?" It was mean and uncalled for, but it didn't stop him from saying it.

"No," she said coldly. "Do you have someone else?"

He didn't answer. She already knew, anyway, he'd never loved anyone but her. Last thing he would do was utter the words.

She blew out a breath. "I meant that it was unfair to let things linger all these years, unfair to both of us."

"Then why did you?"

Shannon looked away. "I've been busy. Medical school, residency."

"Baloney."

Her eyebrows zinged up. "No, it's not."

"Yes, it is, Shannon. Quit lying to yourself and to me."

"I'm… I don't want to have this conversation."

He squared off and stoked up his courage. "Well, we're gonna have it anyway. You are a woman who gets things done, who runs her schedule, owns her choices. You didn't pursue the divorce because, on some level, way down deep, you want to stay married." There. He'd said it aloud, and there was no going back.

She cocked her head, gazing at him, expression unreadable. Should he dare have hope that perhaps his boldness would break down the wall between them?

He waited, hardly daring to breathe, praying she would give him the answer he wanted.

Shannon's stomach twisted, heart beating fast. Her mouth opened and then closed. *You want to stay married.*

The minutes seemed to tick away in slow motion as those blue eyes pierced her to the core. "You're wrong, Jack."

"No, I'm not, but if you want to delude yourself, that's just fine. You called me from the hotel…"

"Because I was desperate."

"No, because you know me, trust me. You always have."

"That's different than loving someone." Wasn't it?

And then he was on his knees, kneeling next to her chair, with an expression so earnest, it made her forget everything but how much she longed to be with him. "Right now, Shan. Look at me, right now, and tell me you don't love me, and I'll leave it alone. I'll hang up my hat and never contact you again after this Dina mess is sorted out, and we'll get that divorce."

"I..."

"Right now."

Her pulse whammed in her veins as he captured her gaze with his. "Tell me that you don't love me anymore."

I love you, I love you, her heart sang. Why couldn't she let go of her self-control and tell him?

She picked up Annabell, though the baby was quiet, and held her close, nearly up to her chin. "Why are you pushing me?"

"I want the truth. Now."

Annabell had nearly fallen asleep. Shannon stroked her head and looked out the window, into the moonlight, into the night.

"Now," he said softly, reaching out and gently tipping her chin. "Tell me the truth. If you don't love me, say so."

"Jack..." she said.

He waited, tense with expectation.

"Jack, I... I can't talk to you anymore. I have my plans, and I have to stick with them. Our marriage is over." Then why didn't her heart believe the words she'd just uttered?

"You aren't a good liar," he said, tracing a thumb over her mouth. "Your bottom lip crimps when you fib."

She clutched his hand, and for a tick, she was overwhelmed with the urge to kiss him. Then she stood, breaking away, baby bundled to her like a shield. He stood, too, watching.

"You are my first love, and I'll always feel something for you, but not the kind of love you need for a marriage." It was the truth she'd told herself daily, for the last seven years. "I was young. We both were. Life has changed. I have changed."

"You've outgrown me?"

"No, I...well, I want different things."

"Uh-uh. You want the same thing, to be a doctor. Well, you know what? You can be a doctor and stay married to me, Shan."

She looked at him full on, and she did not see anger in his face, just a sweet, desperate longing that gradually began to fade, second by second.

"So that's it?" he said finally.

"That's it."

The silence lengthened between them, miles she could not cross, a universe in the few feet.

"You know," he said at last, shoving his hands in his pockets, "someday, when you're done sprinting after everything you think you want—

a thriving practice, accolades, money, success—you're still going to have something missing."

"What's that?"

"Love. The kind your father didn't give you."

She jerked as if she'd felt a hot spark. "And you think you could give me that?"

"No, only God can love perfectly, but I sure would have done my best to love you every day, Shan."

Her mouth opened and closed. In one quick movement, she stripped off the wedding ring and thrust it at him.

"No more, Jack. We're done."

He kept his hands in his pockets. "Keep it."

Breathing hard, she clutched the ring, put the baby on her shoulder and fled without another word.

Shannon cried into her pillow, careful not to let anyone else hear, grateful that Evie, her roommate, had not yet come to bed. Waves of anger and grief washed over her intermittently. How could her choices be so bad? What exactly had she done wrong? She'd had a home in Gold Bar until she'd found another place to belong. She'd embarked on a hasty marriage, born out of a childish need, and then she'd recognized it was a mistake for both of them. She'd loved Jack, but not the way a spouse needed to. She'd grown up, replacing youthful desires with mature ones.

Someday, when you're done sprinting after everything you think you want—a thriving practice, accolades, money, success—you're still going to have something missing.

I'm not sprinting through life because my father didn't love me, she wanted to scream at Jack. It was sheer arrogance on his part to assume he knew what motivated her, what she would or wouldn't miss down the road. Yet doubt carved a trail inside her, etching against her certainty like sand eroding cliffs of granite. Was she running toward her future or away from her past?

I would have done my best to love you every day, Shan.

The rotten thing was, she knew he meant it, every syllable. What kind of fool was she to let him go?

Not a fool. You're going to be a doctor, a great one, and that has nothing to do with Jack or Dad or anything else. She hopped out of bed and shoved the ring into the outer pocket of her backpack until she could figure out what to do with it.

Back in bed, she squeezed her eyes shut and willed sleep to come. Annabell would be up for her middle-of-the-night feeding in a couple of hours. With a start, she remembered that she had not checked her phone since dinnertime. Sitting up again, she fumbled for the bedside table and pressed the cell to life.

The little screen glowed in the darkness. It was not a message from Dina that greeted her, but from Larraby.

Phone number Dina called from hospital matches a former-known cell for Hank Brown, AKA Pinball. He's her brother. Call me.

Shannon sat up, the covers falling away.

Hank Brown. Dina's brother was the leader of the Aces. How could it be true when Dina was considered property of the Tide? When they'd heard rumors that Pinball's people were out to snatch her? She called Larraby's cell.

"If she's made contact with her brother, Pinball," Larraby said without preamble, "he's going to come into town, gunning for the Tide. Have you heard from her?"

"No, not yet."

"When she calls you, you have to loop us in."

"She's done nothing wrong." She heard him wham a stack of papers down in frustration.

"You don't understand the gang thing, do you? They are all about territory and pride and vengeance, wrapped up in a nice fat layer of macho. The Tides are on Ace territory, and if Dina tells brother dearest about how she's been mistreated, they will come looking for payback, and they will not care about the collateral damage."

Shannon could not muster an answer, so Larraby continued.

"Or worse, if Pinball can't forgive his sister for going to the Tide in the first place, there may be truth to the fact that he's trying to snatch her and hand her over to them. Keep his sister's blood off his own hands. Either way, it doesn't end well for her."

"It makes no sense. Why would she have connected with the Tide in the first place?" Shannon said. "Her brother's rival gang?"

"Rebellion, probably. Falling out with the brother. What better way to get back at him than to find a home with his enemies?"

Shannon rubbed the spot between her eyes, where a headache was threatening to take hold.

"If she calls you, you have to let us know," he repeated.

"What will you do to her?"

He was silent a moment. "Nothing."

"But you'll arrest her brother."

"As soon as I see the first sign of violence. It will be the only way to stop World War Three."

"Then the Aces will blame Dina. They'll think she led her brother into a trap to help the Tide."

"That's not my problem. She made her decisions. She's got to live with them."

Shannon's gaze drifted to the baby, sleeping peacefully with her little hands tucked up under her chin. "Annabell doesn't deserve to be caught in the middle."

"Then bring her to me. We'll get her into protective custody."

Tears pricked Shannon's eyes. She knew it was the best thing, the safest thing, for the infant. Her heart ached at the notion of losing contact with the baby. It was a thunderclap to her soul to recognize the truth; she loved that little infant, the baby who demanded every bit of her intellect, patience and compassion. She loved a baby who wasn't hers. With her career and her life in jeopardy, she loved a child the way her father never could.

The tears trickled now. Annabell had changed her in a way she could not fully understand in that moment. Larraby's next words jarred her from her wonder.

"And another thing. Mason's been sniffing around here in town. He left a couple of hours ago, but not before he got some answers to his questions."

"Answers about what?"

"He was asking the old-timers at the café about the Thorns, their ranch." He paused. "Got

Jeb talking, and he can't stop once he's got an audience. Meg said he blabbed to Mason all about the fishing lodge."

Shannon's stomach knotted. "Oh, no."

"If that's where you are, Shannon, you'd better get out. Now. I have to go." He clicked off.

Evie opened the door, eyes rounding in surprise to find Shannon staring at her phone.

"Bad news?"

She was already reaching for her backpack and the diaper bag. "We have to get out of here. Get Jack and Keegan."

"Is it…?" Evie's question died away as the phone began to vibrate in Shannon's hand. She punched the button and answered.

"It's me," Dina said. "I'm here, and I'm ready to take Annabell back."

FOURTEEN

Jack came running at his mother's call, crowded near Shannon, with Evie at his elbow. Shannon put the call on speaker.

"Dina, why didn't you tell me that your brother is Pinball?"

Jack's jaw dropped. "Pinball? As in the leader of the Aces?"

A bad connection made it hard to hear Dina's reply. "How'd you find that out?"

"Never mind how. The point is we did, and you didn't tell us."

"I wasn't sure he'd talk to me at first. We had a pretty bad fight two years ago. That's why I ran to the Tides. It was stupid, but it's okay now. I told him I'd explain everything once I got Annabell back. He's going to meet me."

"You can't trust him. He's either going to deliver you to the Tide or kill you himself."

"No, he won't. You'll see. I'm on a bus, about a half hour away."

"Away from where?" Shannon demanded.

Jack listened to the background noise. Static? The sound of an engine? He could not tell. Two words punched through the white noise.

"The inn."

Shannon almost lost her grip on the phone. "You can't go there. The Tide's people are still in town. They'll…"

"What?" Dina's voice cut in and out. "I don't know what you're saying. I'll be there in a little while. Once my brother meets Annabell, everything will be okay. I can't wait to see her."

"Dina, no…" Jack said. There was no response, only dead air.

With a shaking finger, Shannon clicked off the phone. "There's going to be a bloodbath. We have to call Larraby. My mother…"

Jack dialed Larraby's number on his cell. While he waited to get through, he spoke to her. "Call your mom and uncle to warn them."

Shannon dialed, but there was no answer. "It's going to voice mail. They have the phones on silent for the night."

"No cell phones?" Evie asked.

"They've never gotten comfortable with them."

Jack tried to keep the fear off his face. Her mother, uncle and the guests would be helpless lambs in a slaughter.

Keegan popped his head in the door. "We've got a problem."

"We've got dozens of them," Shannon snapped. "What now?"

"Cruiser and his guys are coming up the mountain. They're about fifteen minutes out."

As the nightmare intensified, Jack took the phone from Shannon and disconnected.

"There's no more time. Keeg, take Annabell and the women in the car. You can make it down the service road before they arrive. Call Larraby on your way."

"What about you?" Keegan said.

"I'll ride Lady, trail Prince behind."

"No, Jack," Shannon said. "You should come with us."

He didn't dignify the suggestion with a rebuttal. "Go."

"You can't go loping off by yourself with the Tide on their way up."

His gut tightened to iron. "There is no way I'm leaving two horses here for the Tide to lay their hands on. End of discussion."

"Hurry, then, Jack." Evie scooped the baby from her crib and headed for the door. Keegan, snatching up his rifle, followed her.

Shannon trailed after Jack as he took his hat from the peg and zipped on a windbreaker.

"This is crazy. What if they catch you? You'll be slow, trailing a second horse."

He didn't answer, so she grabbed at his arm. "I'll ride Prince."

"Uh-uh," he said, brushing her off, shouldering his rifle. "You'll go in the car."

She gave him a full-on, chin-up, eyes-wide stare. "I won't."

He glared at her. "Knock it off, Shannon."

"I'm coming. If you don't want me riding, I'll be hiking along behind you."

He spoke through gritted teeth. "You don't want to be in my life, remember? You just said as much."

"I got you into this mess, and I'm going to see it through to the end."

"Unnecessary. I'm a big boy. I don't need you trying to take care of me out of a sense of guilt."

"Not guilt. I promised. For better or for worse, until our marriage is dissolved."

"It's not really a marriage, not a real one."

"It's a contract. I'll honor it until it's null and void. I owe you that much."

"Don't do me any favors. This isn't a debt to be repaid."

"To me, it is."

"Shannon Livingston, you're nuts."

"Shannon Livingston Thorn, for another few

days, at least." She checked her watch. "And now we've wasted four minutes arguing."

He opened his mouth, closed it, opened it again and finally spun on his heel and marched toward the door. "It will take me a few minutes to saddle the horses," he said over his shoulder.

She nodded. "All right. I'll tell Evie and Keegan and meet you at the shelter."

He stalked off without bothering to answer.

The thought of Shannon riding Prince down a steep mountainside swarming with bikers intent on killing them made his blood run cold.

For better or for worse had just taken on a whole new meaning.

He forced himself to take it easy as he saddled Lady and Prince. No need to let them feel the tension that slammed through him.

Pinball.

The inn.

Cruiser.

And Shannon riding behind him through it as if they were best friends or something. Was she trying to torture him by ending things one moment and insisting on following him the next? When the horses were saddled, he was no more at ease than he had been, especially when Shannon showed up wearing Keegan's baseball cap and a slicker two sizes too big she'd swiped from the closet. She looked so ridiculous, he had to laugh.

She fired him a haughty look and took the reins from his hand. They led the horses out of the fenced area. "Trail's rocky in places, but wide enough."

He offered her his cupped hands, and she climbed up into the saddle. "Is it wide enough for motorcycles?"

He swung onto Lady. "I'm hoping not to find out."

They rode to the trailhead.

Lady's ears pricked. Motorcycles? He didn't stop to listen, but pushed on past the tangle of shrubbery, until they cleared the trail. He set a quick pace, and Lady seemed just as eager to leave the mountaintop as he was. On the way, he tried to calculate the timing. Keegan, Annabell and his mother would be halfway down the mountain, Keegan taking the logging road, which would steer them away from Cruiser and his men. Jack hated the thought of what Cruiser and his cronies might do to the old cabin.

At least they won't be able to touch my horses. Shannon was keeping pace on Prince, though she was not at ease in the saddle. His mind ran ahead to the inn. If Pinball showed up, he'd likely bring some people with him, in addition to the three already there, even though he would probably not be expecting to run into the Tide.

But when he did…

He prayed Keegan had gotten word to Larraby to send police protection for Oscar, Hazel and the guests. Shannon had briefly filled him in on Larraby's call, and he agreed that the safest thing for Annabell was to be far away from any gang altercation. Would the baby wind up in foster care, or be returned to Dina to live under the protection of one gang in place of the one that sought their lives? Rain drove into his cheeks, adding to the sting. Little Annabell. What kind of life was that for her?

He ducked under a dripping branch and held it for Shannon to go by. She nodded a thanks to him. Lady's ears pricked again, and he felt her tense beneath him. Three seconds later, he understood. The sound of a motorcycle cut through the rainfall.

He wheeled Lady into a sharp turn.

"This way," he shouted to Shannon. She stiffened and then urged Prince to follow. He was confident that Prince would stick close to Lady, and he hoped Shannon's skills would be up to the task as they moved down a steep slope, branches clawing at them.

The ground was slippery, but he let Lady pick the path that provided the best footing. They moved quickly, but certainly not quietly. There was no way to move a two-thousand-pound animal through dense foliage without making some noise. He prayed the falling rain would be enough to mask their progress.

When they'd gotten to a dense pocket of trees, he stopped. Prince hunkered up close to Lady's side.

"Are they following?" Shannon breathed. Her skin was pale in the watery moonlight.

He was about to answer, when an engine rumbled to their left. The biker had left the trail and was coming after them.

Urging Lady into motion, he headed for the thickest clump of shrubbery he could spot. It was a hundred feet away, so dense, it rose nearly ten feet high. Lady took the ground easily, but Prince was more cautious. He urged both horses along with his words, as best he could, but Prince had stopped, ears back, balancing uneasily from foot to foot.

He turned Lady and came alongside Shannon, taking the reins from her hand. "Just hold on. I'll lead him."

Foot by foot, with the sound of the motorcycle growing ever closer, he guided Prince into the foliage. They'd just passed through the clawing wet screen when the motorcyclist rumbled to the spot they'd just vacated.

Jack slid off Lady and helped Shannon down. He handed Lady's reins to Shannon and took hold of Prince's bridle, stroking the horse. "It's okay, boy," he whispered.

Shannon gripped the reins and peered through the branches. "It's Viper," she breathed.

"Cruiser probably sent him up the back way. Guy's smarter than he looks."

Viper cut the motor and got off his bike. He stood there. Listening.

One whinny or snort from the horses would give them away.

Rain snaked down the back of his windbreaker, his mind searching for options. If Viper discovered them, they'd have to flee, but with Prince so skittish… He decided if things went south, he'd force Shannon onto Lady with him and cut Prince loose. Prince would run off his panic, find a place to hide. At least Jack prayed that was what the horse would do. What other option was there?

He was still mulling it over, when Viper pulled a gun from his holster and fired.

FIFTEEN

Viper's straight-up-into-the-air shot was meant to frighten them into betraying their location. It worked. Though Shannon was able to contain her own scream, Prince whinnied in fright, bucking against Jack's restraining hand. Prince's startled reaction carried easily on the night air.

Viper smiled and turned in their direction, the gun still in his hand.

"Come out, come out, wherever you are."

She kept silent, though every nerve shrilled. Jack gave Shannon the reins, eased to his horse and freed his rifle, putting his mouth to her ear.

"Ride Lady out of here as soon as Viper's distracted."

He put a hand to the branches.

"Don't show yourself," she whispered, grabbing for his sleeve.

Jack looked at her as if she was speaking another language. "Not gonna shoot a man unawares."

She wanted to shake the crazy noble streak

clean out of him. "Jack, be reasonable. Viper wouldn't hesitate to shoot you in the back."

Jack quirked a smile. "Guess that's why I'm a cowboy and not a biker."

"Don't..."

But he'd already stepped through the branches and into the misty hollow.

Shannon gaped. Of course, that was exactly what Jack would do, the big dope. He wouldn't even consider wounding Viper just the tiniest bit from a place of concealment. No, this was going to be another John Wayne moment. Shannon frantically tried to think of something to use as a weapon. She went to Lady's saddlebag and began to paw through it.

Shannon kept one eye on the action. As Jack cleared the foliage, Viper whirled to face the gun at him.

"Throw down your rifle," Viper said.

"Nope," Jack replied.

"Then I'll start shooting into these bushes. Gonna kill me a woman and some horses, I figure."

"You'll be dead before you get off a shot."

Shannon continued to plunder the neatly packed saddlebag.

Viper laughed again, but there was something uncertain in it now. "You ain't that fast, Cowboy."

"Possibly not, but my brothers are."

Viper's eyes shifted to the tree line, the crag of rocks, the nearby ravine. "You're bluffing."

"Maybe. Then again, maybe my brothers are out here, right now, with a bead on you. We know these mountains better than anyone." Jack smiled. "And we know how to shoot, but then, you already learned that when you showed up at the ranch. You met my brothers then, didn't you? And at the airstrip? Pretty good marksmen, all of them."

Shannon pulled a flashlight from the bag. Shielding it, she pressed the button. It worked, and it had some heft to it.

Viper's finger tensed on the trigger. "I think you're bluffing."

Jack smiled again. "Then take your shot, and I'll take mine."

"Okay," Viper said. "If that's the way it's gonna be."

Through clenched teeth, Shannon mumbled something—a prayer, she realized—before she turned on the flashlight and launched it. It wasn't a particularly forceful throw, thanks to her shaky grip, but the arc of light sailed through the air and dropped at Viper's feet, startling him into lowering his gun. Jack seized the moment and lunged in, his rifle inches from Viper's chest.

"Bring the rope," he called to Shannon.

Shannon did so, and Jack took Viper's gun and tied him to a sturdy oak tree.

Viper seethed. "You're gonna die, Cowboy."

Jack jacked up the kickstand on Viper's bike. Viper's eyes went wide.

"What are you doing? Don't touch that."

Jack rolled the bike down the slope, until he paused at the edge of the ravine. Then, with a mighty shove, he pushed the motorcycle over. It crashed down onto the rocks below.

Viper unleashed a string of profanity, his face twisted in rage. Shannon used a strip of tape from the roll she'd found in the saddlebag to seal Viper's mouth.

"That's better," she said. "You're making my headache worse."

Jack was shaking his head. "So, what part of 'ride Lady out of here' did you not understand?"

"Oh, I understood it all. I just chose not to do what you said."

"May I ask why?" he inquired.

"You didn't say 'please.'"

He blinked.

She did not wait for a reply, but marched back into the foliage, where she'd tied both horses' reins loosely around a branch. More awkwardly than she would have liked, she put a foot in one of the stirrups and climbed up on Prince, before Jack could offer her a hand.

He stood for a long moment, staring at her. Angry? Incredulous? Perhaps the tiniest bit appreciative that her initiative had spared them any grievous injury? She'd never know as he eased onto Lady and urged her back out onto the trail. Prince fell in behind, and they hurried down the mountain.

Lady and Prince were easily convinced to keep a brisk pace when they reached the bottom, and it was another fifteen minutes before they pulled up at the ranch. Jack led them to the pasture, where he unsaddled them and administered a hurried rubdown and a bucket of feed apiece.

"Good work out there, Lady." He gave Prince an extra pat. "And you, too, boy."

He and Shannon hustled back to the house, and his mom met them at the door. "Larraby's on his way to the Nugget."

"Annabell…" Shannon said.

"She's fine. Asleep." She turned to Jack. "Keegan and Barrett left for the inn ten minutes ago."

Jack's breath hitched. His brothers were charging into the fray. They were competent and afraid of nothing, but the Tides had an army behind them who didn't play fair. An army, minus one, he thought, as he pictured Viper tied up to a tree. He'd get around to reporting it to the police when he had a minute. One less gun in the battle, he figured.

"I have to go," Shannon said.

Jack noted the tremble in her voice and didn't try to dissuade her. Instead, he grabbed the keys to the SUV, and they sprinted to the vehicle. He dialed Keegan's number on the way, and his brother's voice came through the car speaker. Jack heaved out a silent breath as they merged onto the main road.

"Pulling up now," Keegan said. "No sign of Larraby. Looks quiet."

He accelerated. "We'll be there in—"

The sound of breaking glass drowned out Jack's words.

"Keegan," Jack shouted.

"Tides just rolled in," Keegan hollered over the din. "They're smashing up the place."

Sirens blared over the line. "Cops are here. Gotta go."

"Don't get in between—" Jack got only a few words out before the connection was ended. Shannon squeezed his forearm in a death grip as he floored the gas pedal. In less than ten minutes, they were skidding into the parking lot, just behind Keegan and Barrett, who got out of their car. Keeping low, they raced to Jack's vehicle. Jack was more than relieved to see them both unharmed. He noted the three motorcycles, which had been toppled, their leather seats slashed.

"Cops ordered us back," Barrett said. "Tides figured out the Aces were here somehow and trashed their bikes."

"Someone tipped them off?" Jack said.

"Looks that way," Barrett said. "No sign of Dina."

Jack heard the passenger door open, and before he could shoot out a hand to restrain her, Shannon was out of the car and running for the inn.

"Shannon," he yelled, but she did not even slow. He sprinted after her. A squad car was parked near the inn's front steps, lights whirling. A window exploded, and he realized the shots had come from the new unit, where the Aces were staying. Return fire erupted from behind a patio wall. He caught a glimpse of one of Cruiser's men ducking down behind the bricks. They must have turned immediately around when they found the fishing lodge unoccupied.

A flash of movement to his left. Tiffany ran toward the trees for cover. He remembered her earlier warning.

Your business brought the Tide onto our turf. That's gonna start a war with the Aces... Pinball's not gonna back down without blood.

But Dina was Pinball's sister. If she was here, waiting to make contact with her brother, would he really risk a shoot-out that might kill her and her baby? *Yes*, he thought grimly. His insane need to defend his territory from the Tides would trump everything, especially if he had no intention of forgiving his sister in the first place for joining up with his enemies. Gang ties trumped blood kin any day of the week.

Jack spotted Shannon, who was crouched low and sprinting toward the front door, and he took off after her. He got as far as the lobby, when someone hooked an ankle around his and toppled him to the floor. Fists up, he was about to defend himself properly, when he recognized Larraby, forehead sweaty and mouth bracketed in hard lines.

Larraby clenched a handful of his shirt. "What's the matter with you?"

"Shannon…"

"I couldn't catch her before she ran upstairs. Stay down. Last thing I need is another person shot."

Another person? The hairs on the back of his neck stood on end. He leaped from the floor, ignoring Larraby's protest, and vaulted toward the spiral staircase. The window in the parlor disintegrated as bullets punched through, and Larraby returned fire before shouting to his deputy via the radio.

Jack took the stairs two at a time and reached the top to find Oscar with his rifle leveled at Jack's chest. He pulled up. "Boy, am I glad to see you. Larraby told me to stay in my room, but I heard you barreling up, and I thought it was those bikers." They both flinched as another gunshot ripped the night.

"Where are Hazel and Shannon?"

He stabbed a finger down the hall. "Gonna keep watch at the window. Cover Larraby and his boys if I can."

"My brothers are out there, too," he said. "Careful, huh?"

Oscar flashed him a mischievous grin. "Ain't shot one of you Thorn boys yet, have I?"

Jack would have laughed if he hadn't been so eager to get to the women. He raced to Hazel's room and knocked. "It's Jack Thorn," he yelled. Trying the knob, he found the door open. Hysterical crying greeted him as he pushed into the dark room.

"Hazel?"

He groped for the light switch, the sobs spurring him on. Finally, he flipped it, activating an ornate lamp covered by a stained-glass dome. The weak light revealed Hazel, lying on the floor, her cane tossed across the room. He ran to her, dropping to his knees.

"Jack," she gasped.

"Are you hurt?"

"No. No, I'm okay." Tears ran down her face and her fingers clawed his hands. "Please, please help her."

Then his senses whispered a message, cold air bathed his face, teasing ripples of fear into his body. The adjoining door in the back of the room was open.

"Where's Shannon?"

Hazel couldn't answer for the crying that shook her. He slammed through the door into the adjoining room, shouting her name. It opened onto a narrow staircase, a back exit from the second floor. Empty. He was about to plunge down it anyway, when a noise brought him to the window. The glass was half gone, shattered by a rock or bullet.

He stared down into the night, thinking his ears had tricked him. Shannon was inside somewhere, hiding.

Down in the courtyard, he saw Cruiser locked into an altercation with a shadowed figure. The moonlight caught the moment as Cruiser dealt a glancing blow, which sent his opponent to the ground. Jack stared, his heart in his throat as Cruiser hauled the limp figure over his shoulder and jogged toward the road. The long dark hair of his victim hung like a shadow over his gang colors.

Shannon.

SIXTEEN

Forcing a sense of control he did not feel, Jack called his brothers. "Cruiser's got Shannon. Heading for the back road." Then he shouted for Oscar, who burst into the room.

"Sis," he said, easing himself next to Hazel with a groan. "What have they done?"

"She's all right. Just shaken. I have to go. They've got Shannon."

With a strangled cry, Oscar thrust his rifle into Jack's hands, his plump fists damp with sweat. He was breathing too hard to get any words out, but he didn't have to say it anyway. Jack was already experiencing enough rage and panic for the both of them.

"Keep the rifle," Jack said. "Stay here until the cops tell you it's safe."

He pounded down the stairs, past Larraby, who was handcuffing a bulky man in Ace colors, shouting for him to call an ambulance for Hazel. There were six squad cars parked every which way outside the main doors. Two biker Aces were on the ground, hands cuffed behind them. Another was strapped on a stretcher. The police must have driven the bikers from the main house and were now going room to room, guns drawn, looking for victims and bikers. The tide of battle had turned, but not for Jack.

He saw no sign of Cruiser on the main road, but he knew that the guy wouldn't be able to ride his motorcycle with Shannon unconscious. Sprinting back to the parking lot, praying he would not be shot by an amped-up cop, he practically dived into the front seat of his SUV. Barrett and Keegan wheeled in next to him in the truck, and Barrett shouted out the window. "Cruiser hot-wired a car from the lot. Took off east, away from town."

"I can cut him off at Mare's Crossing," Jack shouted. Not waiting for a reply, he gunned the engine and flew out of the lot.

You let them win. You let them take her, his gut screamed at him. Through sheer force of will, he fought down the despair. He'd stop them, get Shannon and Dina back. It was the only scenario he'd allow himself.

Mercifully, there were no other cars around as he charged up the highway and jerked the SUV off onto a side road. Why this road? It was not well-known to outsiders, with no quick access to the highway. What if they were wrong? What if Cruiser had headed in an entirely different direction?

Trust your brothers, he reminded himself. If Barrett said this was the direction they'd taken, he'd believe him. He was doing a solid seventy miles per hour, and still saw no sign of them. He was considering pulling over to text his brothers, when he caught the tiny glimmer of a taillight in the distance. Dropping the phone, he put the pedal to the floor. Ahead was the hot-wired sedan that had been stolen from a guest at Hazel's inn. Hope leaped to flame. He pressed the SUV as hard as it would go, until he was yards from the rear bumper.

He didn't see Shannon in the car. She was probably lying on the seat, being bounced around like a stone in a violent flood. His jaw clenched so hard that his teeth ground together. Cruiser would pay for every bruise, every bump, Shannon had to endure.

Now he was closing the gap even more, the SUV gained ground on the stolen vehicle with every passing moment. He could make out the shadow of Cruiser's blocky frame, tensed behind the wheel, his skinny cohort in the passenger seat, turning to assess Jack's approach.

Jack pulled to the passenger side and began to edge closer. He prayed he could force the car off the road, into the nearby grassy field. Then it would be a standoff, but his brothers were somewhere close behind, and they would provide suitable backup. Three Thorns against two bikers. That would work just fine, unless Cruiser planned to use Shannon as a human shield. Nerves twitching, he pressed harder.

His front bumper was inches away now from the rear door of the car. Almost there. He caught the profile of a woman's face and almost lost his grip on the steering wheel.

The face that looked back at him, eyes wide with terror, was not Shannon.

Confused, he looked again into the back seat. The captive, mouth covered with duct tape, cradling his unconscious wife, was Dina Brown.

Shannon jolted back to consciousness and tumbled to the floor of the car. Her mouth was taped, and her hands were bound together with a dirty bandanna. Flashes of memory assailed her. Running into her mother's room, finding her on the floor, a flash of movement and then her arms twisted sharply behind her. Fighting and tussling down the stairs and outside, until a blow to the head knocked her out. Struggling to regain a place on the seat, she sucked in a breath through her nose at the sight of Dina, also gagged, hands tied together, trying to help her back up onto the seat.

Dina's meeting with her brother, Pinball, had either not taken place before the violence at the inn, or he had allowed Dina to be handed over to the Tide. Her heart ached for her mother, her uncle, for the patrons at the inn, all the innocent people who would be caught between the rival gangs in their quest for vengeance. She had a feeling she and Dina were going to be whisked away, back to Southern California, and handed over to the Tide, once they extricated themselves from Gold Bar.

She silently prayed a thank-you that they had not brought Baby Annabell into this disaster. Her thoughts surprised her. Another prayer offered up to God, in whom she had never put any stock. Was it weakness? She'd always relied on her own smarts, strengths and determination. In that moment, she realized she had precisely zero control over her own life or Dina's. She was helpless. If God was the loving entity Jack insisted He was, why was she drowning in fear? Was she left again in the hands of a father who would not love her the way she craved?

A whimper from Dina cut at her. She gripped Dina's hands as tears trickled from the young woman's eyes. She offered the only comfort she could, a touch, an unspoken promise that they'd ride it out together. In spite of her terror, that touch of one hand to another comforted her beyond words.

As they clung together, Shannon tried again to formulate some sort of plan. Cruiser and the man in the front seat were focused on an approaching vehicle. It took her a moment to realize the figure silhouetted behind the windshield was Jack, gripping the wheel, bearing down on them.

Her heart squeezed, and a thrill of hope almost choked her. If they could get out, tumble clear of the car somehow… She tried the handle and found it locked. With a thrust of her chin, she commanded Dina to try her side. Also locked. The car must have one of those kid-safe overrides that kept the doors secure until the driver released them.

All right, Shannon. Plan B. She would disable Cruiser, wrap her bound hands around his eyes and at least slow him down enough that Jack could reach them.

As she readied herself, Dina caught her eye and shook her head, her brows furrowed in fear. Shannon's desperate act might very well result in a crash, but she did not see any other choice. If Cruiser got them away from Gold Bar, it would be death for both of them.

She leaned forward just as the skinny man in the front seat turned around and shot out a fist at her. Recoiling in time to avoid the blow, she tried to suck in enough oxygen to steady herself before trying again.

This time, as she eased forward, Cruiser's cohort was completely focused on the oncoming vehicle. Jack was so close now, she could see him in the side mirror. His expression was a mask of grim determination. The trust was so clear. He loved her, and she'd walked away from him.

As she lifted her hands again, the passenger pulled a gun from his pocket and aimed it at Jack's front windshield.

"No," she screamed against her gag, lunging for him instead. Flailing awkwardly to reach him, she struck at the back of his head just as he loosed the shot. It ruptured Jack's windshield with a crack. Shannon watched in horror as she lost sight of Jack behind the spidering glass. The SUV suddenly jerked out of control. It toppled over, spinning in sickening spirals that sent pieces of debris careening in all directions. Over and over, it tumbled, until it came to a stop in the grass upside down, smoke pouring from under the hood.

Shannon stared out the rear window, horrified.

Jack, you have to be all right. You have to be.

She stared hard, every atom in her being hoping to see the shadow of his strong form sit up and push his way out of the car.

But there was no movement from the SUV.

No movement at all.

She realized that Cruiser had slowed and was looking in the rearview mirror.

"Got him," he said with a laugh.

She hardly heard. Dina squeezed her hand, tears flowing freely, but Shannon was too overwhelmed at what she'd seen to cry.

"Meeting place is fifteen miles from here," Cruiser said.

"We gotta get out of town, man. Staying around makes us sitting ducks. Cops will be looking for us, and those Thorn brothers. Youngest one almost patched into the Aces, you know. He's all kinds of wild, and when he figures what we just did to his brother..."

"We wait for the exchange, Skids."

"Why?" Skids fired back. "We got what we want now."

"Because I said so," Cruiser barked. "She's got to die by her own people, or the Aces will gun us down one by one."

By her own people? Shannon roused enough to try to digest the meaning. Slowly it dawned on her. They'd gotten it wrong. The Ace informant wasn't working to hand Dina over to the Tides.

Someone in the Aces had negotiated with the Tide to ensure their right to murder Dina Brown.

She's got to die by her own people. Was her own brother eager to end her life himself because she'd gone to a rival gang? His own sister meant so little?

She looked into the young mother's terrified eyes. Had they murdered Jack, too?

Or was he gravely wounded?

Again, she had no control, no ability to do anything but put her bound arms around Dina and try to press the message home to her.

I'm here.

And I'm not going to leave you.

It was illogical, this deep-down need to comfort. Science could not explain the root of love and compassion. There was no biological motivation, no identifiable practical reason why one person should care for a stranger.

Or why someone should give his or her life for another.

Tears burned now, blurring Dina's image, but still Shannon held on.

And maybe that was where God was, in the love, the craving of it, the sharing of it and in the grieving for its loss.

She pulled Dina close and cradled her as she'd done to Dina's daughter, their tears mingling together as the car drove on.

SEVENTEEN

Jack wasn't sure if his eyes were opened or closed. The SUV had landed on its wheels, the top dented in, and the front end crumpled, bringing the steering wheel up close and personal with his chest.

Images rolled slowly through his fogged brain, until one stabbed at him with such force that he hollered. A memory of a woman draped over Cruiser's shoulder. "Shannon!"

"Stay still," a deep voice said.

He recognized it as Barrett, who was yanking at the crumpled door frame, which caused the vehicle to shudder. He wanted to tell his brother to stop because the impact was making his ribs spark with pain, but it seemed too much effort to get the words out. The glare of the truck's headlights nearly blinded him. Blinking, he saw someone climb in through the window, crouch next to him and pull a knife. He tensed.

"Just me. Seat belt's jammed." Keegan sawed

at the restraint. He paused when Jack groaned, and then he ran his hands along Jack's skull and extremities. "You breathing okay, big brother?"

Jack managed a nod. "I'm all right."

Keegan called out to Barrett. "He's bleeding some on the forehead, but nowhere else that I can see." He finished sawing through the seat belt. "Man, that was a spectacular crash. I counted three flips."

Three flips. It had felt like a hundred. He remembered the shot that must have ruptured his tire. He'd been so close, so close to reaching Shannon.

"Ambulances are tied up at the inn," Keegan said, "so I'm gonna be your medical provider for the time being. Good thing I had three weeks of summer camp first-aid training before they kicked me out. You may call me Medic Keegan."

He finally managed to get some words out. "I'm doomed."

Keegan taped a bandage to his forehead. "Glad your dim wit is still functional. Stop moving, would you? It's like trying to saddle a bucking horse."

"Shannon," he said.

"We called the cops with the license plate and their direction," Barrett said, still yanking on the driver's door. "Mom, Dad and Shelby are already making calls to the neighboring ranchers, asking them to keep a lookout. They won't get far. Police have roadblocks set up between here and the highway. They're gonna have to hide out, and we'll find them." With a screech of metal, the doorway gave under Barrett's powerful yank.

He groaned as Barrett grabbed his arms. Keegan lifted his legs, and together they slid him from the SUV and put him on the ground, on top of a blanket.

He tried to get up. Keegan held him down, without the use of much force, since Jack felt wobbly as a newborn foal. Concentrating on breathing, he tried to assess the damage to his body. Fiery pain in his ribs, a slow ache building in his wrist, a myriad of twinges and aches.

"Can you feel this?" Keegan said, tapping his left boot and then his right.

"Yes, and it hurts, so knock it off."

Keegan grinned. "Cranky patient."

Jack tried to shove the blanket off and sit up, but Keegan held him down. He wanted to push Keegan away, but he was shivering with shock.

"We'll find her," Keegan said softly, holding him in place. "But not you, not now. You're going to the hospital."

"I'm gonna clobber you when I get my wind back," he snarled.

"Uh-huh. I'll try to control my terror."

They managed to bundle him up in the blanket and load him in the second-row seat of the truck. His head was crammed against the passenger-side wall, and his boots scraped the driver's side. But anything that would get him out of there, where he could start tracking Shannon, was tolerable.

He bit back the urge to howl as his brothers ignored his demands to skip the hospital. They drove away from the crash site, away from Shannon.

Knowing she was in Cruiser's hands was the most excruciating pain of all.

Shannon tried to track how long they'd been driving. Thirty minutes? Forty-five? The road was curvy and sloped, and the area was heavily wooded. Cruiser stopped occasionally to peer at his cell phone at the map displayed there, and Skids shot him a doubtful look.

"There's nothing around but shrubs," Skids said.

"Keep looking."

They rolled slowly on the rough road, until Cruiser slammed a hand on the wheel, making Shannon jump. "There. I knew it." He guided the car down a perilously steep path that she would easily have passed by without noticing. It took them to a dark clearing, where there was a small cabin nestled next to a pond. Shannon tried not to be swallowed up by the panic that gripped her as she surveyed the isolated spot. No help for miles. No way for the Thorns or the police to find them.

Jack. The crash, the impact. It was as if she could feel it in her own body. How many catastrophic car-accident injuries had she treated in her emergency room? Some had happy endings, families restored, loved ones so relieved, they dissolved into tears and threw their arms around her. Some victims were left with ruinous injuries that would damage their quality of life forever. Some never emerged alive from the hospital, despite her best efforts.

No. Not Jack.

Cruiser parked the car behind the cabin and ordered them out. Shannon had long since peeled away the tape from her mouth and did the same for Dina. Cruiser and Skids had been so focused on finding the hiding spot, they had not noticed or cared. Now it was a nonissue. *There's no one to hear our screams*, she thought. No traffic noise or the comforting sound of a dog barking. Only the mournful chorus of frogs and crickets.

Skids herded them along the weed-covered walk. The front door was unlocked, and he nudged it open with his boot. The door swung wide, and a half dozen startled bats flew out.

Dina screamed, and so did Skids, which made Cruiser laugh.

"Real tough guy, Skids. Get them inside if you can handle that. I'm gonna make a call."

Grumbling, Skids shoved Shannon inside after Dina, almost toppling her on the warped wood floor. Skids reached for a light switch, but there wasn't one.

"No electricity," she said.

"I knew that." He turned on the flashlight on his cell phone, which illuminated a small square space with a table, two chairs and a stone fireplace. An alcove served as the kitchen, with some overhead cabinets and no appliances. A closed door indicated there was another room, a bedroom perhaps. There was no indoor plumbing that Shannon could see. *Rustic* did not even come close. She could tell by the look on Skids's face that roughing it was not to his liking. It wasn't much up her alley, either, but she wouldn't show it. A memory of a long-ago day with Jack popped into her mind. When they were newly graduated high schoolers, he'd taken her up to a spot in the mountains, basically a lean-to, atop a steep bluff, where he and his brothers used to camp.

Check out the view, he'd said, spreading his arms to present the rolling hills.

But she'd been staring at the chink in the

wood floor where she'd been certain she'd seen the rump of a disappearing rat. *I think there are rats.*

He'd laughed, swept her up in his arms and kissed the top of her head as he again presented the view. *There, now. All safe.*

All safe. The way she'd always felt with Jack. For a moment, she could hardly draw in a breath, so she forced away both the long-ago memories and the recent horror of the crash.

Cruiser pushed through the door. "Can't get a signal. I'll hike up to the road later. For now, we'll sleep here until we're contacted."

"Since when do we wait for orders from the Aces?" Skids demanded.

Cruiser's face went hard as iron. "Shut up, Skids. At the end of the day, we get what we want, plus a nice chunk of change for our troubles."

"If word ever gets out that we made a deal with the Aces..."

Cruiser grabbed him by the neck. Skids clutched at his throat, but Cruiser's look was pure fury. "Not the Aces, just one Ace."

Just one. Hank?

"No one's gonna find out, Skids. Girl's gonna die. We're gonna get the payoff and go home." He shoved Skids backward, until he stumbled against the wall. "Maybe," Cruiser said with a laugh, "we'll even get ourselves the baby, too. T.J. would treat us like royalty if we brought his little girl back to him."

"No," Dina said. "You stay away from my baby."

Cruiser silenced her with a look. "Don't you get it, honey? You're gonna die. Dead girls don't get to dictate terms." He smiled, and a wail of despair erupted from Dina. Shannon pulled her back and into a hug.

"Shhhh," she whispered. "Don't let him know how scared you are." Dina gulped and rubbed her eyes with her jacket sleeve.

"You two make yourselves useful and see if there's anything to eat," Cruiser said.

He took a seat at the table, facing the kitchen, gun placed in front of him to send the message. *You live until I decide you don't.*

She propelled Dina into the kitchen space and began to prowl through the cupboards. Shannon could hear Dina's stomach rumbling.

"How did they get you?" Shannon whispered.

Dina winced. "I finally found a contact of my brother's. Handed him all my cash to give me a number, and I sent Hank a text. I didn't tell him much—just that I was in trouble and needed his help. We agreed to meet at the inn."

Shannon shot a look at Cruiser, who was fiddling with his phone. "Did you tell anyone you were meeting him?"

Dina shook her head. "No. I bummed a ride to town. I was walking up to the courtyard, looking for Hank, when Cruiser grabbed me from behind. He was expecting me."

"Dina, someone in the Aces wants to kill you before the Tides get the chance, and they're willing to pay." She paused, remembering Tiffany's comment at the inn. "Hank sent his girlfriend to find you, to get the baby before the Tides did."

Her eyes rounded. "To protect us."

"That's what she said, but I don't believe it."

"Hank wouldn't hurt me," she said. "He must have heard that I was in town before I managed to contact him and sent his girlfriend. He wanted to keep me safe." Then she chewed her lip. "If word gets out I was with the Tide, the Aces would all want to kill me for sure. Without my brother's protection…"

Shannon was far from convinced that Hank was an ally, but she let it go. "You should have told us who your brother was," she murmured, shooting another look at Cruiser and Skids. "Do they know?"

She nodded. "I don't think so, but they've been plenty rough with me. They also know that Annabell is my baby, not yours. I think Mason told them." She sniffed. "They've been taunting me about how they're gonna give Annabell back to T.J. after I'm dead." Her stomach growled again.

"When was the last time you ate?"

She shrugged. "I had a candy bar yesterday, and a lady at the café gave me a bottle of water."

In one of the musty cupboards, Shannon found three cans of baked beans, along with a rusty can opener. She cranked open the baked beans and emptied two of the cans into some cracked bowls, after wiping them out with the hem of her shirt. She stuck in spoons and plopped them onto the table, in front of Cruiser and Skids, without a word.

"That's it?" Skids said. "That's not enough."

"There's one more can, but we're going to eat it," Shannon said.

He glared at her, fingering his gun. "I don't think so. Bring it here."

"I won't."

Skids fired his gun into the ceiling. Shannon flinched. Dina screamed. Skids and Cruiser laughed.

"Get me the food," Skids grunted.

Shannon stared him down. "She's hungry. If you want to shoot, go ahead, but you'll be welching on your deal with your Ace, won't you? They want her alive." Shannon faced Skids full on, her heart rampaging in her chest.

Cruiser dug into his beans. "Quit being a

baby, Skids. Eat your beans and leave the little girls alone."

Stiff with fear, Shannon whirled on her heel and walked back to the kitchen. There was only one bowl left, so she poured the beans in and grabbed two spoons, rubbing them as clean as she could on her shirt. They crouched on the floor and took turns spooning up the beans. Shannon stopped after a few bites.

"You finish," she told Dina.

"No, we can share," Dina said, but the hunger still showed in the lines of her face, the tension of her fingers clutching the spoon.

"I had soup earlier. I'm okay. Eat."

Dina nodded and wolfed down the rest of the beans. They sat there on the floor together until Skids began to yawn.

"I'll take first watch," Cruiser said. "You can sleep in the car."

Skids nodded.

"Where will we sleep?" Shannon said.

"I don't care if you sleep at all." Cruiser propped his feet up on the table, the gun in his lap. "But if you try to get away, I will shoot you." He smiled. "We're not getting a dime for you, Doc, so it don't matter when I do it."

When I do it.

The truth hit her hard as a hammer blow. Dina was part of the deal. Shannon was not. Cruiser would kill her when his business was concluded, or maybe before. There was no way he would leave any witnesses.

The minutes ticked away, sending her further and further into despair.

EIGHTEEN

Jack didn't waste time with an official hospital discharge. As soon as his fractured wrist was splinted, he escaped, his brothers chiding him all the way out the exit door.

"There's no word on Shannon or Dina," Barrett said as he drove back to the ranch. "Be sensible. You can't do anything for them until we get an idea of where they went, especially with a busted wrist."

He ignored Barrett, staring at Keegan from the back seat. "You can find Dina's brother, Hank. Gang name's Pinball."

Keegan raised an eyebrow. "Their leader? I'm not exactly in the good graces of the Ace's head honcho. I washed out, remember?"

"No, you realized you were being an idiot, and you didn't want to throw your life away by joining a gang," Barrett said.

"Thanks for the tender words, Bear," Keegan said.

"You have contacts still, people you can ask," Jack prodded.

Keegan studied him. "I don't know if they'll talk to me, but I'll try in the morning."

"Now."

"It's almost 1:00 a.m. Not optimal time to elicit cooperation."

"I don't care."

"Right. What I meant is, I'll try right now."

"How's Hazel?"

"She's gonna be okay. She's distraught about Shannon, so they had to sedate her."

Jack swallowed hard.

"You did everything you could, Jack," Barrett said.

Jack closed his eyes. "Not enough, but I will get her back. What's the status at the inn?"

"Lots of superficial damage to the structure. One guest requiring stitches for a bullet that grazed his shoulder. Bikers all fled, except the few that were arrested. It's a blessing that no one was badly hurt. They've had to close up until this thing is sorted out."

Pain gouged at Jack, inside and out.

"Okay," Keegan said, clicking off his phone. "I left a message with someone who should know how to get word to Pinball. Now all we can do is wait."

"No, we can start a search party."

Keegan grinned. "A posse? Straight out of the Western?"

"Something like that."

"Keeg and I can handle it," Barrett said. "You…"

But Jack waved him off, tensing against the pain as he wriggled the phone from his pocket. It was mercifully undamaged and maddeningly void of messages.

He stared at the blank screen, thinking about Shannon, willing her to get word to him somehow. *Where are you, Shan?*

One slim hope throbbed deep down inside Shannon. The phone, her cell. She'd tucked it in an inside pocket of her jacket, and neither thug had thought to search her. Maybe she could get a message out, a text that might send in spite of the spotty cell coverage. But the cabin was so minuscule, Cruiser would detect the tiniest flicker of light from her phone. She could wait for him to fall asleep, but she was not sure how much charge was left in her depleted battery.

"I'm thirsty," she said.

"We all are," Cruiser snapped.

"I can get some water at the pond. Boil it to make it safe."

Cruiser licked his dry, cracked lips. Cocking his head, he considered her words. "All right.

I'll holler out to Skids to let him know, so hopefully he doesn't shoot you." He pointed the gun at Dina. "But she stays."

Dina sucked in a breath and gripped Shannon's hand. "Don't leave me here alone."

"I'll come back." She smoothed Dina's hair. "I promise, I will come back."

"If you don't," Cruiser said, "I'll hurt her. Bad."

Dina clutched her fingers until the bones ached. "Please."

Again, she realized the odd truth that she would risk her own safety and freedom before she abandoned Dina. She had not known she was capable of such self-sacrifice, and it both scared and bemused her. Where did that well of deep emotion come from?

Perhaps God.

And perhaps, too, it had been nurtured by a mother's love and the devotion of a man who had shown her again and again that she was worth saving, worth loving. Thinking about Jack made her throat clog with pain.

Cruiser strolled to the smudged window. "Got a great view from here, Doc. One whiff of disobedience, and you know what will happen."

If he found out…

She thought of what Jack would say, how

he'd hold his chin up and quietly defend what he knew to be worth protecting, worth loving.

"I'll be back," she said again to Dina, grabbing a dented pot and pushing the door open. The night air was cold and heavy with the scent of spring. Nerves screaming, she walked away from the cabin, allowing her vision to adjust to the near-total darkness.

Clouds drifted across the moon as she pushed into the tall grass. It whispered against her legs as if it had secrets to tell. The ground became mushy under her feet, and she picked her way closer and closer to the glittering edge of the pond.

She crouched behind a clump of cattails and fished out her phone. Just one message to Jack. Just one.

It came to her in a sickening flash that even if Jack had survived the crash, his phone might not have. She'd text a message to both him and Larraby, if she could, but how could she communicate where they were? She had no idea what road, or even what direction, they'd taken away from the Gold Nugget, since she'd been unconscious for part of it and terrified for the rest.

All she needed was one second to take a picture and send off a text.

She pushed her fingers into the grass at her feet and found a stone. Without giving herself time to think, she launched it into the air. It plunked on the roof of the small cabin and bounced down. Three seconds later, the front door of the cabin was flung open, and in that precious gap of time in between, she took a photo of the cabin and sent the text. Her phone showed two bars of charge left, enough, she knew, enough.

Her rush of triumph was crushed a moment later when the screen notified her.

Message sending. The little bar eased its way across the screen and stalled.

She had to return to the cabin, and if someone texted a reply back, Cruiser or Viper would surely hear it, but it was their only chance.

Message sending.

It was still not sent when she heard the sound of booted feet crashing through the cattails.

NINETEEN

Jack's dark mood eased a bit as he greeted the group gathered in the kitchen of the Gold Bar Ranch before sunrise, on Tuesday morning. They all held cups of coffee, the table sporting the remnants of the cinnamon bread his mother had put out. He said hello to Ken Arroyo, Barrett's father-in-law, who had an arm slung around his daughter, Shelby. Barrett stood protectively nearby. Drake Gregory, a friend from a neighboring town, was also there, as well as Oscar.

"Hazel's resting comfortably, still sedated. Her cousin Jenny is staying with her so I could come here and give you an update."

Arroyo's and Gregory's horses were hitched to the post out front.

Jack could not resist kissing the top of Annabell's head as she nestled in his mother's arms. "We're gonna get your mama back, Little Bit," he whispered into her fuzz of hair. The rabbit he'd given her was tucked next to her tummy.

His mother must have snatched it up in their flight from the cabin. The baby responded to his kiss by skimming her petal-soft fingertips over his chin, a touch that made his heart swell. So fragile, so innocent. This seven-pound critter had gotten right down inside him in the few days he'd been her pretend daddy. And Shannon, too, had seemed to be falling just a wee bit in love with Baby Annabell. That notion had to be put right away immediately, since any thought of Shannon amped up his emotions to near-panic level. Reluctantly, he moved away from Annabell, standing, rather than enduring the discomfort of folding himself into a sitting position.

Keegan was on the phone in the family room, trying to get a response from the contact he'd looked up to secure access to Dina's brother, Pinball. The frown on his face suggested he was having no success.

Larraby joined them, pushing through the crowded room after Tom opened the door for him.

Jack didn't waste time with pleasantries. "Did you pick up Viper near the cabin, where we tied him?"

"Yeah, he's in custody and not talking. Big surprise."

"He might not have known about the plans at the Gold Nugget anyway," Barrett suggested.

"Cruiser and the other guy may have cooked up their own plan after you hog-tied him."

"What do you have worked out?" Drake said. They all crowded around the table to scan the spread-out map.

"I've marked it," Shelby said. "Everyone has a search area."

"You can stop right there," Larraby said. "This isn't the Old West. None of you have the authority to go off with pistols cocked."

"Rifles," Ken said, "and we all have permits to carry them. We're not breaking any laws."

"These bikers are armed and dangerous," Larraby said.

"So are we, and they made the mistake of taking one of our own and the woman she's protecting." Drake's expression was grim. "We can't ignore that."

Jack felt a swell of gratitude. He couldn't ask for better neighbors.

Larraby glowered. "Let the police handle it."

"On horseback, we can go places you can't." Ken squeezed Shelby's shoulders. "We'll divide the search areas and check in by phone."

Shelby tapped a corner of the map. "I've chalked out four grids, one for Barrett, my uncle Ken and Drake, who will be on horseback, one for Keegan on his motorcycle."

"Where's mine?" Jack demanded.

Shelby looked at him. "I didn't think, I mean, with your broken wrist…"

"It's fine."

There was an awkward silence, and he felt the weight of all the eyes in the room.

"Well, I'm going to say it since I'm the pregnant lady, and that gives me permission. You should stay here, Jack. You were just in a bad accident," Shelby said.

"Not too bad since I'm still upright and breathing." He took his rifle from the closet. "I'll make my own search grid, call in if I see any sign of Cruiser."

"No, you call the police in," Larraby said. "We're not going to have you all rushing into a gunfight like you're a bunch of cowboys."

All the men in the room stared at him. "We are cowboys," Jack finally said, "and we take care of our own." He meant to push by Larraby, but the man put a hand against his chest.

They squared off, and Jack thought his heart was going to pound right out of his chest if Larraby delayed him a minute longer. "Unless you're going to arrest me," he snarled, "get out of my way."

Larraby held there for a couple of seconds. "Don't do anything dumb," he said before he slowly stepped away and shifted his gaze to Evie. "I'll get a squad car over here to pick up the baby as soon as I can. Have her ready in a couple of hours."

Evie clutched the baby tighter but did not reply. Jack wanted to grab Annabell to his chest and fly her someplace where no gang members would ever touch her. Instead, he allowed himself a moment longer to look at the small bundle, perfect and oblivious to the chaos building around her.

"I'll bring your mama home," he repeated silently. "And Shannon, too."

A split second after Shannon shoved the phone in her sock and sloshed some pond water into the pot, Skids grabbed her shoulder and hauled her to standing position.

"You're hurting me," she said. "Cruiser told me to get water."

"Something hit the roof of the cabin and fell off on top of my car. A rock, I think."

"It wasn't me."

His eyes narrowed, and he grabbed her by the waist and patted her arms and torso. Her cheeks went hot, and she tipped the pot so it doused him. He sprang away from her with a curse.

"Now look what you made me do," she said. She scooped up more water and walked gingerly away from the pond, praying Skids would not decide to search her again and discover the phone in her sock.

Back in the cabin, Cruiser brushed off Skids's suspicion. "What's she gonna do out here in the boonies? Go back to sleep, you pinhead. I'm gonna hike back up to the road in an hour to get a phone signal, but I need some sleep first, so keep it down."

Dina greeted Shannon with a brilliant smile. "You came back."

"Just like I promised." She forced a happy tone. *Message sending.* Her plea for help was stuck in limbo, a desperate call that might never be heard, like a note in a bottle tossed out into stormy seas.

Shannon had only a foggy idea of how to use the dusty cookstove, but to her surprise, Dina took charge. "My grandma had one. I lived with her when my mom took off."

"How old were you when that happened?"

"Six. She met some guy who could feed her habit, and off they went. Left me and Hank with Grams." Dina smiled.

"Grams would have thrown in some dried potato peels to keep the creosote from building up." Dina lit the wood, Shannon heaved the pot onto the stove and they sat down by the crackling warmth. Cruiser had watched their efforts for a while, but now his head was on the table, and he appeared to be asleep.

An idea came into her mind. She just needed a signal, and Cruiser was the one who could get it for her. Heart beating faster, she helped Dina feed more wood into the fire, which crackled and puffed until, twenty minutes later, the water bubbled enough to kill off any harmful bacteria. Using her jacket as a makeshift oven mitt, she eased it off the heat.

She poured some water in a mug, where it began to cool quickly. Her plan was half-crazy, she knew, but better than nothing. She took the mug and approached the sleeping man. When she heard another soft series of snores, she eased the phone from her sock and slid it into the outside pocket of his vest. Dina looked at her in complete puzzlement. Cruiser must have felt her proximity because he jerked awake and stood with such haste, his chair fell over with a crash.

"Whaddya doing?" He waved the gun from her to Dina.

"I brought you some water. It's still warm but almost drinkable."

He looked as though he did not quite believe her, and her heart thunked so hard, she almost choked as he yanked at his vest. Any moment he might discover her phone in his pocket, where he would unwittingly carry it to the road, if her desperate scheme worked. Instead, he righted his chair, the gun never wavering. "You sit back down over there by the stove, Doc, with the little tramp."

"She's not a tramp," Shannon said, but she complied, sliding to the floor, next to Dina, who she hoped had wiped the astonished look off her face.

Skids banged through the door. "I can't sleep. All these frogs and crickets, and it's cold out there."

"Take your turn inside," Cruiser said. "I'm going to hike up to the road to get a signal, see if there's a message." He shot a hard look at Shannon again. "I don't like dragging this thing out. Sooner we can finish the job and get our money, the better."

Shannon watched them go, struggling to keep her breathing steady. She'd taken a huge risk, and she might just have ruined them both.

"Lord," she prayed. "Please." She had not prayed since she was a very little girl, and the words seemed rough and rusty on her tongue, but Jack always said God listened to all prayers, big or small, so she added one more thing.

"Lord, please let Jack be alive."

TWENTY

Jack headed to the barn, ignoring the pounding ache that started in his wrist and slammed through his body with increasing intensity. Keegan intercepted him.

"Tonight," he said. "Midnight, at a parking lot in Rock Ridge."

Jack sucked in a breath. "We meet Hank?"

"We meet Hank's guy. He'll vet us, and if we pass muster, we'll be taken to Hank."

"And if we don't?"

Keegan arched an eyebrow. "Then things are going to get ugly fast."

It was something. Did Hank's willingness to meet mean he really did want his sister safe, or was he ready to kill anyone who had aided her perceived treachery to the Aces?

Jack offered Keegan a weary thanks and headed for his father, who held Lady's reins. She was saddled and ready. "Your mother wants you to eat something and take pain meds. Larraby's sending a man to move Annabell to a safe house. It's temporary, until they can get her into the care of social services."

Social services. His heart lurched. With a groan he was unable to stifle, he climbed into the saddle.

The sun rose into a sky that was puffed with cotton-candy clouds and backed by a sizzling blue. No rain. It would help the search. He was grasping at straws, and he knew it.

Leading Lady, he tried to let the rhythm of the horse soothe his nerves. Lady's ears wiggled at the burble of the creek that bisected their property. It took him sharply back to a time long ago. Shannon was mired in college applications and financial-aid forms, and he had taken—no, practically dragged—her away for an afternoon of fishing at the creek, something she had never done before. After much coercion, she'd agreed to drop a line into the water. He'd caught nothing, but it didn't matter one whit. He was intensely, completely and utterly satisfied to sit next to Shannon. To be with her, to listen to her talk of her plans and watch the sun tease the glossy chestnut glimmers from her hair was all he needed. She'd caught a fish, an impressive trout with speckled sides that he helped her haul out onto the sunbaked rocks.

You just caught our dinner, he remembered he had said, jubilantly.

She'd looked from him to the trout. *We have to let it go*, she'd said, wide-eyed.

But you catch 'em to cook 'em, he'd said through his laughter. *That's the whole point of fishing.*

Then came her tears, welling from some dark and wounded place, spilling down her cheeks. *Please, Jack. Can you get the hook out without hurting it?*

So, he'd looked into those tender, tear-filled eyes, and he'd immediately set about removing that deeply sunk hook and tossing the prize fish back into the river, where she'd watched until it vanished under the water.

Heaving a sigh, she'd smiled and blushed, wiping her cheeks with the back of her hand. I'm sorry. *It's just, I... I didn't want it to die.*

And with his half-melted heart beating hard, he'd pulled her close, kissed her sweet mouth and decided then and there that he was going to make her his wife. His wife. It had in no way turned out like he'd thought, but he was not sorry that they'd gotten married, not sorry at all. It pained him heartily to think that she felt differently.

His phone buzzed, and he pulled it out. Would it be a message with an answer? Would it be an answer he was prepared to hear? It was a photo, dark and grainy, slightly blurred, as if it was taken in a hurry. A bolt hit him when he realized it had come from Shannon's cell phone. He shouted and slid off Lady, texting a reply. Where? Are you okay?

The screen supplied no answer.

His father and Keegan came running. "It's a text from Shannon to me and Larraby. She's alive. She sent a picture of where they're keeping her."

They all three stared at the picture as his mother joined them.

"Some kind of cabin," Keegan said. "I don't recognize it."

His mother's face lit up as she peered at the screen. "Wait a minute. That glimmer there in the window. That's a reflection of water, a river—no, a pond."

Jack's whole body went cold and then hot. "I know where she is," he said.

His mother nodded. "The pond up by Ridgetop Cabin. It's been empty for years, except for the hikers who use it sometimes. I'll get word to the others and call Larraby to tell him we identified the place."

He put a hand on her sleeve. "Give us a half-hour head start."

She looked troubled. "Jackie…"

"If Cruiser smells the cops…" He could not

finish aloud. If Cruiser got wind of police involvement, he would kill Dina and Shannon before he attempted an escape.

No witnesses.

No mercy.

No time to lose.

Shannon awakened a couple of hours later, her muscles cramped. Dina's head lay against Shannon's shoulder. Skids was snoring. She wished she knew the time. *Late morning? No, early afternoon*, she decided. The cabin door flung open with such a crash that Skids shot to his feet. Dina startled awake with a cry of surprise.

Rage shone on Cruiser's face. He held up her phone. "What did you do, Doc?"

Dina climbed stiffly to her feet.

Shannon tried to move away from the young woman, in case Cruiser was going to shoot her. She didn't want Dina caught in the cross fire.

"I slipped my cell phone in your pocket while you slept," she said, chin up.

"So, what's the big deal?" Skids asked, rubbing a trickle of drool from his chin.

"She took a photo of the cabin and texted it to Cowboy Jack, only there wasn't a strong enough connection, so…" Cruiser trailed off.

"So I put it in your pocket, and when you hiked up to the road, where the signal was stronger, the text sent automatically." She smiled. At least for one moment, she had bested Cruiser. "You sent my message for me. Thank you."

He rushed at her, grabbing her throat. She grappled with his fingers as he squeezed off her oxygen. Dina batted at him, but he pushed her away. "I didn't find your phone until just now, but you know what, smarty-pants Doc? It's not gonna matter anyway." His face was inches from hers.

Skids swore. "Cowboy people know where she is? When did the message send?"

"An hour ago. I just now found her phone in my pocket. Cowboy sent a follow-up text, but of course Doc here couldn't respond."

A follow-up text? Jack was alive. Heart soaring, she pulled again at his fingers.

His nails cut into her neck before he shoved her to the floor, where she lay gasping. "Think you're so smart, don't you? By the time the posse gets here, we'll have handed Dina off to our Ace, gotten our money and you'll be dead. Our contact will be here any minute, so pack up your stuff."

He aimed a kick at her, but she scooted back until her shoulders hit the edge of the counter, sending a knifing pain through her lower back. Dina clutched her around the shoulders. "We're gonna keep her just in case Cowboy does show up. Cowboy won't shoot if his wifey is in the way. As soon as the exchange is made, she'll die." He laughed, yellow teeth showing. "You don't feel so smart now, do you, Doc?"

Shannon did not give him the satisfaction. She kept her gaze on her knees, concentrating on breathing in and out through her swollen throat, focusing on the thought that made her whole body prickle with joy. Jack was alive. He'd gotten the photo an hour ago. With every fiber in her being, she believed that Jack would take on any enemy, no matter how formidable, to help her. Skids had finished packing up his few belongings from the car.

"Car approaching, stopped up at the main road," Cruiser said. "Now it's turning down the drive."

Shannon caught a glimpse of a battered Chevy. Not Jack, nor any of his kin, as far as she knew. She shivered.

Skids wiped sweat from his forehead. "Sure it's not cops?"

"It's our Ace. Cover me from inside, just in case. Put them in the bedroom. Windows are stuck shut. I checked. When I give you the all clear, bring them out."

Skids prodded them into the bedroom and slammed the door shut. Shannon heard him ease the front door open, probably taking up position there. Immediately, she ran to the window and tried to tug it open. Cruiser was right. It might as well have been welded into place. Frantically, she searched for something to break the glass.

The only thing that might work was an old wooden chair.

"How can we break the window without anyone hearing?" Dina asked.

"We can't, but we're out of time and options." She grabbed the chair. "Once I smash it, kick the glass away and get out. Run as far into the woods as you can. Get to the road when it's safe. You'll be okay."

"What about you?" Her eyes were wide.

"I'll follow if I can."

"Shannon," Dina said, snatching up her hands. "I… I don't deserve all the risks you've taken for me and the baby."

Shannon looked at the girl, who had delivered herself from one gang to another, made herself property and birthed a baby into a world of violence and degradation. A girl who, like Shannon, had not been loved the way God meant.

And how had such a selfish woman, the brilliant doctor who turned her back on her husband and pursued prestige, come to put her life on the line for this young lady? She did not know, but she knew her selflessness came from somewhere else. Maybe there was a true Father smiling down on her now.

Tears crowded her eyes, and she squeezed Dina close. "You deserve a chance to be loved and to be a mother to Annabell."

"Thank you," Dina said.

Shannon gently pushed her away and picked up the chair. "Ready?"

With a convulsive swallow, Dina nodded.

Shannon recalled the times Jack had tried to teach her how to hit a baseball. With all the strength she could muster, she smashed the chair into the glass.

TWENTY-ONE

Jack had just secured Lady to a tree set back from the road and grabbed his rifle, when he heard the sound of breaking glass. He hurtled down the wooded slope that paralleled the drive to the cabin, with Barrett and Keegan right behind him. From his left, Drake shouted something, but he couldn't make it out.

The Chevy that idled in the driveway kicked to life, rocketing into the grass, in an effort to turn around. Barrett aimed a shot at the tire. It pinged off the rear fender.

Shots erupted from the doorway of the cabin. He returned fire, but kept his aim low, so the bullets plowed into the wet ground. No way would he risk hitting Shannon or Dina. He wasn't sure if they were in the car or the cabin, but the shattering glass had come from the back of the house. Something in his gut told him it was the women.

"Gonna get to the back," Jack hollered to

Barrett, who began to lay down cover fire. The Chevy was still bumping and rolling over the grass. He caught a glimpse of Drake and Ken Arroyo, keeping their horses to the safety of the tree line and seeking positions to get off a clean shot at the vehicle.

As he rounded the corner of the building, a bullet grazed his hat. He dropped to the grass and belly crawled behind a tree in time to see Cruiser fire wildly and sprint away along the side of the house.

He leaped into pursuit and dived behind a teetering woodpile as Cruiser squeezed off two more shots, which scoured chunks of wood from the sodden logs.

Keegan threw himself down beside Jack a moment later. "Car made it out of here."

"Did you see—"

Keegan cut him off. "One driver. No passengers visible."

Visible.

Cruiser shot again, the bullet making them both hunker down.

"What's the plan here, chief?" Keegan said.

"I'll draw his fire. See if you can get around to the other side of the cabin, and we'll go at him from both fronts."

"And by 'draw his fire,' you mean do something reckless and stupid, like…"

Jack poked his head around the topmost log and began shooting wide, while he tried to ascertain where Cruiser was hiding.

Keegan sprinted away.

Cruiser hollered, "Throw down your rifle, or I'm gonna kill her."

Jack froze as Cruiser eased from behind the trees with his arm wrapped around Dina's throat. She clutched at him, her mouth open to scream, but nothing coming out. His gun was pressed to her temple.

"Come on, Cowboy. Throw out your rifle."

"Not gonna work," Jack said. "You're outmanned, and cops are coming."

"Then I guess I got nothing to lose."

Jack was a good shot—excellent, in fact—though not as skilled as his twin. What were Dina's chances of surviving if his aim went wide? His mind shifted to Shannon. Where was she? There was no sign of movement from inside the house, but he didn't have much of a view through the busted-out window. Tires skidded on gravel from somewhere in the front of the property.

Keegan might have a better line of sight, but he was not as good a marksman, and they both knew it. Sweat dampened Jack's temples.

"No more time, Cowboy. Guess I'm gonna have to shoot her."

"Then you'll die before the bullet clears the gun."

Cruiser laughed. "Always wanted to go out in a blaze of glory."

Jack's grip tightened on the rifle.

From behind the overgrown junipers, a figure rose up, swinging a sturdy tree branch. Shannon. Her expression was not frightened, but resolute, her dark hair tangled with leaves, as she arced the branch at Cruiser's head. Jack was so startled, he almost missed the opportunity. Her aim was off, and the branch smacked ineffectually against Cruiser's shoulder, but it was enough to distract him into loosening his hold on Dina. Jack took the shot.

The bullet entered through Cruiser's right clavicle and spun him around, knocking him to a sitting position, against the side of the cabin. Keegan erupted from the bushes, shoving Dina behind him and wrenching the gun from Cruiser's hand.

Jack felt as though he should drop to his knees right there and then and thank the Lord Almighty. Shannon appeared unharmed as she knelt next to Cruiser, stripping off her jacket. He watched in utter amazement as she folded the material and pressed it to Cruiser's bloody shoulder. He approached cautiously.

"Hold this on the wound," she said to Jack, efficient, every inch the doctor.

He stood there, mute.

"Here," she ordered again in such a tone that he crouched next to her and pressed his palm to the fabric against Cruiser's wound. Cruiser groaned, eyes closed, teeth gritted.

She prodded around Cruiser's back, moving him just enough to check behind him. She huffed out a breath. "A through and through. I don't think it caught anything important."

Jack kept up the pressure, but he could not stop staring at Shannon. She was as in command in her medical element as he was in the horse arena.

"Shan, are you okay?" he said softly. "Did he hurt you?"

"No, not much."

Not much? His teeth clenched together.

"Too hard," Shannon said, touching his hand that was pressed against Cruiser's wound. "Less pressure."

With effort, he eased off, and she bunched up Dina's offered jacket behind Cruiser. "Why didn't you just shoot him in the leg or something?"

He goggled. "Because that's not how it works."

"Well, you might have killed him," she said.

He had no comeback for that.

Ken Arroyo raced up. "Drake's tracking the car. Cops just arriving." He glanced down at Cruiser. "I was a medic back in my army days. Let me help."

He took over for Jack, who eased off. Shannon rose to her feet, finally coming around to face Jack.

"You might have killed him," she repeated, face very white.

He took a breath. "I'm sorry I shot the bad guy?"

"Me, too, because now he's going to need a nice, cushy hospital bed when he should be going straight to a horrible, dark cell…" Her voice rose with each syllable. "…in a damp tower, with only bread and water, because…" Her breath came in and out in bursts, and tears began to roll down her smudged cheeks. "Because I thought he'd killed you." Now the sobs came in stuttering waves, cries racking her body as she hugged herself.

Jack sighed. "No, honey. I'm okay," he said, folding her into his arms, her shudders quaking as he laid his cheek on the top of her head. "Everything is going to turn out all right."

Now that she was free.

Now that she was safe.

His wife, if only for one more day. With the tip of his finger, he angled her face toward his, and their lips met. Her mouth was warm and yielding. He fancied the kiss was filled with longing and love, but it was probably only his heart speaking for both of them.

Sighing, he eased his head onto her shoulder and let the nearness of her put his fear to rest.

Larraby met with the makeshift posse as the ambulance rolled away with Cruiser inside. Skids was in custody, refusing to say a single word, other than profanities. The car with the traitorous Ace had escaped into the woods.

Shannon had finally stopped crying. To her mortification, she clung to Jack so long and so hard that the medics had pressed for her to be transported to the hospital, also. Jack's kiss had surprised and thrilled her. She could not seem to convince herself that it had really happened. She and Dina had finally escaped the Tide, and the whole ugly affair might truly be over, the missing Ace aside. She could return to her life, her career and the real world the next day.

After a quick flight to Los Angeles, she would put on her scrubs and box up her wedding ring for good this time. That was still her plan, wasn't it? Then why was her heart breaking into pieces at the thought of leaving Jack? And why did the kiss keep intruding on her thoughts? Best not to dwell on it now, she decided. Noticing that Dina was marching resolutely to Larraby, Shannon forced herself away from Jack and joined them. Jack followed anyway.

"I want Annabell," Dina demanded of Larraby.

"She's safer in protective custody."

"No." Dina shook her head. "I want my baby."

A shadow of disgust crept across Larraby's face. "Your brother is probably the one who wants you dead and sent someone to collect you from Cruiser. The father of your baby and his people will kill you if you ever set foot in Southern California. What kind of life is that for a baby?"

Shannon touched Dina's back. "I can help you get started somewhere else, somewhere safe for Annabell."

Dina shook her head slowly. "I'm going to meet with my brother, and then I'll decide what to do and where to go, but it's my choice, unless I'm under arrest."

Larraby shook his head. "T.J.'s been released from the hospital, and he's not making a formal accusation against you. You're not safe, you and the baby, but you're right. I can't keep you from taking her. We'll go tomorrow."

"Now," Dina said.

"I'll have someone take you." He stalked away from them to a fellow officer.

Dina sagged. "I don't know if my brother will trust me enough to meet me. He might think I was in on the ambush. I just need to explain, and then I'll take Annabell and go."

Jack rubbed a smear of dirt from his chin. "Don't do it, Dina. It's not safe for you or the baby."

"I know, but I have to tell him. I have no family except him, and I want him to see his niece, just once. Then I'll go, but I don't know how to find him." Her eyes were pleading. "My brother was the only one who ever loved me. He won't let me down now. I am going to keep looking for him by myself. If you won't help me, I'll have to go to the Aces."

Shannon understood. She'd already grilled Jack about her mother and Uncle Oscar until she'd been satisfied they were all right. At that moment, it seemed to Shannon that family ties might be the only kind that mattered.

Her own thoughts surprised her, considering she did not even know where her own father lived at that moment. But she had been given a spectacular mother, uncle and—she cast a quick glance at Jack—husband, for a while at least. That had to be a God thing. He tied people together with bonds that strengthened instead of strangled.

"I'll help you find him," Shannon said. "At least until I have to leave tomorrow, but I won't help you put Annabell in danger."

Dina hugged her, and they clung to each other, bonded by the baby they both loved and the ordeal they'd just survived.

Jack blew out a breath that made them both break away and look at him.

His face was pained. "I know where he is. We have a meeting arranged at midnight, but it's not safe for you two to go."

They nodded their heads.

"Whoever Pinball sent, if it was him, is still at large, or it could be some rogue Ace working on their own, without his knowledge. So you get why it's a bad idea for you to join us to meet him?"

Two more nods.

He rubbed a hand over his jaw, which sported a yellowing bruise and a five o'clock shadow. "And you're going to come anyway, aren't you?"

"Yes," they said in perfect unison.

"That's what I thought," he said with a groan.

TWENTY-TWO

At dinnertime, Jack, Dina, Annabell and Shannon assembled in the abandoned kitchen at the Gold Nugget. Jack figured it was as safe a place as any, since the inn was temporarily closed down. Hazel would be released from the hospital in the morning. He read their body language plain as day during their visit to Hazel in the hospital: Shannon torn about leaving her ailing mother, and Hazel determined that her daughter would do exactly that, in order not to lose her emergency-room internship. It ended as he thought it might. Plans were made for Shannon to see Hazel once more before her 3:00 p.m. flight back to Los Angeles.

Now busily entrenched in the Gold Nugget kitchen, against his protests, Shannon rubbed a palm over her forehead, her eyes shadowed with fatigue. "I tried to convince Mom to let the place stay closed a few weeks, but I didn't get anywhere, of course. I can't get much time off to come help, so I'm strong-arming her into hiring another cook and housekeeper. At least all the bikers have gone elsewhere. Too much police attention, I guess." She was busily scrambling eggs and making toast, while he put on a pot of coffee. He wanted to drink in every detail, from her hair, which collected in a loose bunch at the nape of her neck, to the way her mouth quirked as she surveyed the cooking eggs.

The truth was a hot flame that burned in spite of Jack's strident efforts to extinguish it. He loved his wife. He loved her with as much ardor and tenderness as he ever had, maybe more now that he'd almost lost her in the crazy charade. As a newlywed, he'd believed that love was enough, would always be enough, to keep a marriage alive.

Love, his love, was not enough, and it never had been. The eggs stuck in his throat, and he had to force them down with a slug of too-hot coffee that burned his tongue.

Annabell played contentedly in her bouncy seat, grabbing at her own feet, when she caught a look at them. The shadow of loneliness fell over him with a tarry blackness that pressed away his earlier joy.

After the makeshift meal, Shannon and Dina retreated to empty rooms to shower and change, leaving Annabell with him. When the women were gone, he scooped her from the bouncer and tucked her close, his chin skimming her silk-soft hair as he sang the horsey song again.

More time passed than he'd realized when he looked up to see Shannon standing there in jeans and a clean shirt, her hair damp and glistening from the shower, a wistful smile on her face.

"You're going to be a good daddy someday, Jack."

"And you'll be a good mommy."

The statement seemed to startle her. Her fingers found a stray strand of damp hair. "Maybe," she said. "I was always so ambivalent about ever being a parent, but I don't know. Something about Annabell makes me think I should keep an open mind."

He chuckled as the baby reached out for his chin, grabbing with a look of determination on her perfect bow of a mouth. "Good. Hate to see all that love you've got go to waste." It was the wrong thing to say. She flushed and dropped her gaze to the floor.

"I really am grateful for all the help, the risks you took…"

"No need to thank me."

"You'd have done it for anyone?"

No, his heart said. *Just for my wife*. His insides felt wobbly, so he didn't answer. After another round of the horsey song, he settled into a chair, with Annabell in his lap. "I'll take you to the airport tomorrow, Shan."

He craved with everything in him to hear her say she'd changed her mind. "That's, uh, still the plan, right?"

Her expression went soft as she looked at him. "Nothing has changed, Jack."

He tried to shrug away the feeling that his heart was ripping in two. "Sure."

"I can get myself there."

He skewered her with a hard look. "You're my wife for one more day. Let me at least hold on to that for a few extra hours, huh?"

She opened her mouth and then closed it. "I… I'm sorry, Jack," she said in a voice that was barely a whisper.

So am I, he thought as he looked at the baby. He was only a small fool for falling in love with Annabell, a baby that was never his in the first place. What kind of man could resist the parental tug of caring for a baby?

But he was an enormous fool, a colossal idiot, for allowing himself to fall in love all over again with Shannon.

Shannon's body craved sleep, but her mind would not allow it. Her stomach was in knots at the upcoming meeting, and her heart felt as if it was in tatters every moment she thought of Jack.

She was up and pacing when Keegan arrived in the Thorn-family van at the Gold Nugget, at precisely eleven thirty. Annabell slept through the transfer to her car seat.

"We'll leave Dina and the baby in the van until we're sure the meet is secure," Jack said. "Shannon, stay with her."

Shannon figured there was no point in arguing as they drove to Rock Ridge. She heard enough to know that Tom and Barrett had driven separately and were taking up a position somewhere in the darkness. When they arrived, Keegan parked underneath a streetlight in the parking lot of a machine shop, leaving the keys in the ignition.

"If anything goes south," Jack said, "Barrett and Dad will cover us from the trees, and you drive out of here as fast as you can."

"Leave you and Keegan?"

"That's the idea, yes."

"You'd be killed."

"We're tough." He looked at her then, and she could see the hurt shining deep and clear as the river rocks under the creek where they'd fished so many years ago. *Not so tough*, she thought with an ache. *I hurt him worse than anyone ever could.* How could she explain that her own pain was intolerable? Her craving to stay with him so strong, it almost eclipsed her dream to become a doctor. But if she gave words to her longing, stayed for one more day to be close to Jack, she'd never have the courage to leave. She had to take her own path, to stand up and prove once and for all that she was enough.

There were only a few empty trucks parked near the building. The rest of the spaces were empty. Keegan and Jack walked away from the vehicle and stood silhouetted by lamplight.

Dina unstrapped Annabell from the car seat when she fussed and eased a bottle into her mouth. The rumble of motorcycles made them both tense. Two riders rolled toward Jack and Keegan as both women strained to see.

"Is it your brother?"

Dina peered into the darkness. "The tall one on the left, I don't recognize." She gasped as the other man, muscular, wide-shouldered and long-bearded, stepped off his bike. "It's Hank," she said.

In a second, she'd pressed the baby into Shannon's arms and shoved open the door.

"No," Shannon called as Dina bolted from the van. Shannon hopped out with Annabell to stop her, but it was too late. Dina ran toward her brother, who yanked a gun from his waist. His second in command did, as well.

Jack shoved Dina behind him and stepped between them.

"Easy," Keegan said. "She's just excited to see her brother, man. Take it down a notch."

Hank looked over Jack's shoulder. "Last time I tried to see my sister, I almost got my head blown off."

"So did she," Jack said. "Instead she got kidnapped by one of yours and handed over to the Tide. Was that part your idea?"

Hank glowered, finger still on the trigger. "No way. Only my closest people knew about Dina being back and our meeting plans, and none of them would betray me. None would lay a finger on my sister, either..." He frowned. "Unless I ordered them to."

"Did you? Because she went to your rivals?" Jack shook his head. "You'd consider killing your own sister?"

"Maybe," he growled. Dina flinched. "But I didn't. I wanted to hear her out, that's all. Maybe she set me up so her Tide friends could off me. Was that your plan, Dina? Looking to get even for our blowup all those years back?"

"No, Hank," Dina said, tears trickling. "I'd never do anything to hurt you. I don't know what happened at the inn. I just wanted to talk. I'm sorry. I'm so sorry. We fought all those years ago, and I... I got involved with the Tide to spite you. It was dumb, and I regretted it, but I couldn't get out."

Hank peered at her through slitted eyes. "Heard about your man, T.J., getting busted up. They say you did it. You knock him down the stairs?"

"No, but they blame me. T.J. hurt me plenty, Hank. I had to get away for my baby's sake, but I didn't hurt him."

Hank tensed. "Could be that's just a sob story."

"No," Shannon said, coming a pace closer, but still staying close to the van, in case she had to get Annabell to safety. "I'm an emergency-room doctor. Your sister was beaten over the years. I treated her myself. She tried to get away. She called you from the hospital, remember?"

Hank raised a puzzled eyebrow. "I never got that call."

Dina groaned. "I thought you'd just ignored it."

Hank considered a moment before wagging his chin at his partner, who holstered his weapon. "So why are you here now, Dina? Tides got their go-to guy busted, I hear. If there's a problem in my Aces, I'll take care of it. Got nothing to do with you, and you got nothing to do with me. Not anymore."

Dina walked around Jack's restraining arm and took Annabell from Shannon.

"No," Shannon whispered.

"He's my brother. He loves me." Dina returned to Hank, with Shannon following behind. "Hank, this is Annabell. I came here for your protection, but after everything that's happened, I know I can take care of her better on my own. I'm leaving, but I wanted to say I love you, and I'm sorry, and to show you your niece one time before I go, since I'm not going to come back."

Hank looked from Dina to the baby in her arms. Shannon thought he might have sighed. "She looks like Gran."

"Yes," Dina said. "She does. And she's spunky like Gran, too."

Hank put out a massive hand and touched the crown of the baby's head. "If you had just stayed here," he said, voice much less gruff, "instead of running off to Los Angeles."

"I know," she said. "I made mistakes."

"Yeah," he muttered. "We all did." He stared at Annabell for a moment longer. "Listen, things are messed up right now, and I gotta clean house. You're right to go somewhere to keep the kid safe. I'll help. I'll get you some money and set you up in a place, a secret place. When things get better—" he shrugged "—I'll come and see you, maybe, visit."

Dina beamed a smile that was a mile wide. "I don't want your money, Hank, but I'd like you to visit someday. I really would."

A sprinkle of rain began to fall.

"I'll put her back in her car seat," Dina said, walking toward the van.

"Hank," Jack said, "you have to face the fact that one of your people made a deal with Cruiser to help capture her. Whoever it was tipped them off to her location repeatedly."

"Must have happened some other way. Mason, the cop, maybe was behind it. Dina's my kin. No Ace would dare touch her without my say-so."

Shannon fisted her hands on her hips. "You're going to have to put your bloated pride aside because that's exactly what happened. If the Thorn brothers and their friends hadn't gotten us out, Dina would be dead, and so would I."

"Who you figure?" Hank said, staring at her.

"Tiffany was the one who talked to us."

Hank gaped. "No way. No way she would do anything like that."

"Like I said," Shannon snapped. "Set your pride aside."

He was silent a moment, and she knew he was putting the pieces together. "I hear you and Cowboy stuck your necks out for my sister."

"Yeah, and we almost got killed for it," Jack said.

"Plus, the Gold Nugget Inn's all busted up," Keegan said. "Your people had a hand in that, too."

"I'll put out the word. No one touches the inn

or any of your people ever again, as a thank-you for helping my sis."

"What's your word worth?" Jack said.

Hank stepped up close, practically nose to nose with Jack, who did not flinch. Keegan drew closer, and Shannon held her breath.

"My word's solid as I am. Yours?"

"Rock solid," Jack returned. "If Dina ever needs help, all she has to do is call."

"Why would you do that for mine, Cowboy?"

"Ever heard of 'love thy neighbor'?"

Shannon swallowed hard as the two men glowered at each other.

A grin crept across Hank's face. "Yeah, I think I heard that a time or two."

"I just thought of an idea," Shannon said. "A place where Dina and Annabell can stay, if you are sure the Aces won't touch them."

"I'm sure, but what about the Tides?" Hank said. "Can't trust them for nothing, and they still got a beef with you."

Dina shook her head. "T.J. washed his hands of me and the baby. He thinks we're more trouble than we're worth." Then her chin went up. "I don't want him around Annabell anyway. She's going to grow up without the Tide or the Aces in her life."

Shannon's admiration for Dina washed over her in a bubble of pride, and she knew her half-baked plan to find a place for them was right on target.

Jack started to reply, when a cry whirled them all in the direction of the van. Rain glistened on Tiffany's rain-dampened jacket. It also shone on the barrel of the gun, which she held on Dina with one hand, clutching the baby, face-first, to her chest with the other.

TWENTY-THREE

Shannon's stomach dropped.

"Tiff?" Hank said in disbelief. "What do you think you're doing?"

"Let go of the baby," Shannon shouted. "You're smothering her."

Dina cowered on the ground. "Please, please give me my baby."

Tiffany ignored her pleas, but she kept the gun aimed at Dina's chest. Annabell kicked the blanket away in her efforts to breathe. Her small feet gleamed in the dim light, wriggling faintly. "You're not going to help her, Pinball. You're not going to give her your protection. Once the word gets out that you're helping a Tide, you'll lose all respect."

Both Shannon and Jack moved toward Tiffany. Keegan dropped back, and Shannon knew he would try to circle around for a surprise attack. There was not much time. Tiffany gripped the baby so tightly, her knuckles shone white.

"She's my sister," Hank growled. "And you don't get to tell me what to do. Ever."

"I've tried everything to save you." Tiffany's eyes were wide and crazed in the light of the streetlamp. "When I saw the hospital number on your phone while you were sleeping, I knew it must be from her. I erased the message. Paid some people there to keep tabs on her for me. Soon as I heard a rumor she was in town, I tried to keep her away. I stole her phone, tipped off the Tide whenever I could."

"Why?" Hank demanded.

"Because I knew you'd go running after her, after a Tide woman." Her tone was laced with disgust. "When I found out she was making her way here, I knew I had to stop her, because you'd fall for her sob story. Poor, sad Dina. But she wouldn't give up, just kept on trying to find you. You'll look weak, don't you see, if you take her in?"

His brows drew together. "So, you made a little deal with Cruiser to get your hands on her? What were you gonna do, Tiff? What were you gonna do to my sis?"

"Kill her," Tiffany said. "Because you're too weak to do the right thing yourself."

Jack took another step forward. "Just give me the baby," he said. "Then you can sort it all out with Pinball."

Shannon's heart was thundering as the moments spooled on. Was Annabell getting any oxygen with her face pressed hard into Tiffany's chest?

"Don't you get it?" Tiffany shrieked, with tears sparkling. "I did this for you, so you wouldn't get your hands dirty. If Dina dies, she'll be rightly punished for consorting with the Tide. Those are the rules for everyone."

"Not for my sister," Hank said. He pulled his gun.

"No," Shannon yelled. "You'll hit the baby."

Jack lunged forward. Dina bit Tiffany hard on the wrist. She howled, and Jack threw himself on the gun hand. Shannon had only one mission: to catch the baby before she hit the ground.

She threw her body forward and managed to skid to a stop, just in time to absorb Annabell's fall. Keegan sprinted up and helped Jack subdue the thrashing Tiffany. Barrett and Tom emerged from the bushes to help secure the situation.

"They're my family," Jack shouted to Hank. "Don't touch them."

Shannon moved the baby out of range of the tussle.

Dina was sobbing now. Hank's beefy arm was around her.

"I'm sorry, sis. I never would have thought she'd do something like that."

"I did it for you," Tiffany shrieked. "I did it all for you, Pinball."

Her hollering turned to wails as he shook his head in disgust.

Jack pulled out his phone and called the police, while Shannon examined the baby with shaking fingers.

"We'll take care of Tiffany," Hank said with a hate-filled stare at Tiffany. "She's one of our own."

"No way," Jack said. "She belongs to the cops now, not to you."

"Jack," Shannon screamed, and her own voice cut through the night like a missile.

He jerked toward her.

"The baby isn't breathing," she said. "Call an ambulance."

Jack dropped to his knees next to her.

"Tell me what to do."

"Put a jacket under her, something."

He stripped off his jacket. She lifted the limp body and placed it on the fabric.

"Oh, no, no, no," Dina wailed.

"Quiet," Shannon snapped. "Move her from here, please."

Hank dragged Dina a few paces away. Keegan was on the phone. "Five minutes." He grabbed an umbrella from the van and held it over Shannon and Jack as they knelt in front of the baby.

Five minutes. Jack knew that was far too long to wait. Shannon unsnapped the tiny outfit and put two fingers on the baby's breastbone and pushed quickly in succession.

"Count," she commanded.

"To what?"

"Thirty."

He did, numbering off the compressions, his own heart slamming into his ribs with brutal force. It was as if time spiraled into slow motion and there was nothing but counting and the ice-cold fear in his gut. At the end of thirty compressions, Shannon tipped Annabell's chin back and laid a palm gently on her forehead. Then she breathed into her mouth for two breaths. He watched her tiny rib cage rise and fall.

And the cycle continued, endlessly, rhythmically, until he pushed Shannon away from Annabell's head. "I got it. I'll do the breaths."

She scooted over, and he took a position. Annabell's skull was between his palms, cold and fragile as an eggshell. Shannon took over the counting, face outwardly calm, except for the flare of her nostrils, the intense concentration.

Thirty compressions.

Then he breathed softly into Annabell's nose and mouth. *Come on, Little Bit. Live.* Dina's sobs echoed over the rainfall. He did not dare risk a look at her, did not want to see the sheer terror of a mother watching her child teeter on the razor edge between life and death.

Another series of compressions, and Shannon stopped, bent low over the baby and felt the inside of her outthrust arm for a pulse.

Expression stark, she moved into position to resume compressions, when Annabell jerked, mouth open, eyes wide, body stiff and thrashing. Shannon put her cheek close.

"She's breathing on her own."

He wanted her to say it again, to make him believe that the still, small form had crossed the boundary from death back to life again.

Shannon did not move from her crouched position. Her fingers were wrapped around Annabell's arm, checking to be sure her heart continued to beat.

In the distance, a siren wailed. It was closing fast, but the three of them were locked in an intimate tableau, tracking every precious breath and beat, until the paramedics and police arrived almost simultaneously. Annabell was still breathing unassisted when she was whisked into the ambulance by a pair of medics, and Larraby took custody of Tiffany.

Tiffany glared at Dina as she was led to the squad car.

"You ruined everything. Why did you ever come back here?"

Larraby folded her into the back seat.

Dina broke from her brother's embrace and threw her arms around Shannon. "You saved her," she sobbed. "You saved us both."

Dina swayed on her feet as Hank gently guided her to a police officer who promised to take her to the hospital.

"I'll be right behind you," Hank said.

Shannon sank back to her knees, on the jacket where she had just saved Annabell's life.

"Hey," Keegan said softly as he folded the umbrella. "Rain stopped."

"Yeah," Jack said. He went to his knees, one hand on Shannon's shoulder as she crouched there, staring at the spot where the baby had lain a moment before.

"Shan…"

Keegan stepped back. "I'll call Mama. She'll want to know." He returned to the van.

Jack tried again. "Shannon, let's get you in the van. You did great work here," he said. "Amazing work. I'm proud of you."

She still did not look at him, and he saw she'd begun to shiver. He gripped her hand. "Shan… come with me."

"Wait," she whispered. She gripped his fingers and whispered a broken prayer of thanks.

He pulled her close to him, and together they thanked God for preserving Baby Annabell's life.

Jack could not talk much because of the gratitude that clogged his throat as he helped Dina and Annabell settle into a room at the Gold Nugget Inn. He'd already made mental plans to find reasons to visit the old inn regularly and often. Uncle Jack was ready to spoil Annabell rotten. Hazel was positively beaming, gushing about childcare details for the hours when Dina would work in the dining room and help with housekeeping. Mostly, he figured, she was beaming because there would be a baby to fuss over, maybe the closest she'd ever get to a grandchild. That thought followed him back to the ranch as Shannon sat silently in the passenger seat. Back at home, he tried to settle his spirit by tending to his chores, but even the horses could not soothe him as the hour of Shannon's departure drew closer.

When the time arrived to leave for the airport, he could not find her. She had reportedly gone to lie down, but she was not in the guest room, nor the living room or kitchen. He began to prowl the property.

He finally found her at the fallen tree, the same tree that spanned the creek where she'd caught her first fish and then let it go. She sat there in the mellowing sunlight, her face scratched and pensive. It was the most breathtakingly lovely sight he'd seen in his thirty-two years of living. Her small backpack was on the grass next to her, plane ticket poking out of the outer pocket. The uncertainty on her face broke his heart all over again.

Quietly, he took his place next to her on the log, and she did not seem surprised to see him.

"Decided on some fresh air before I take you to the airport?"

She didn't answer. He wanted to touch her, to hold her, but he was not sure how she would react, and he figured it would just make everything that much more difficult.

"You okay, Shan?"

Shannon continued to stare at the ground. "I don't know."

His fingers itched to reach out. "Talk to me."

"I'm not sure how to correctly capture it in words."

"Let the words come out however they want to. You can put them in the right order later."

Not even a flicker of a smile. Alarm bells began to jangle deep in his gut. Whatever she was about to say was going to change things, and he was not sure he'd like the result. She was leaving; his heart was already cut clean through. What could make it worse?

She got up and began pacing circles in the grass. "Annabell was close to death. Technically, she was dead. Not breathing. No pulse."

He swallowed, recalling the little form, his fake daughter, rain speckling her face, eyes closed. "You saved her."

"I didn't, though."

He was going to interrupt, but he realized she needed to say it, to give voice to whatever was weighing on her soul.

"I didn't save her. Yes, I did the compressions and breaths like I was trained, managed her airway, etc., but…but…"

The wind flicked the leaves above them, sending one to the ground, and she picked it up, twirling it in her fingers, and then sat down again. "But whether she lived or died, that was all I could do, just the steps, the training. The life… or the saving of it…was not up to me."

He cocked his head, mesmerized.

"It was up to God," she finished. "I think I've always known that, but my pride never let me admit it."

"Yes," he said, keeping the joy from his tone. "It's always His decision."

"And He…" Her eyes widened in wonder. "He decided to give me life."

He nodded gently. And what a spectacular life He'd created in her.

She gazed up at the trees, a dark curl edging her cheek. He shoved his hands under his thighs to keep from capturing that strand with his fingers.

"And he kept me alive through this whole miserable experience with Cruiser."

"I'll always be grateful for that," he said softly. "Every single moment."

She did not seem to hear. "So, the life is His, but the living of it, the days and moments are up to me."

"Yes."

She looked so fearful then, he could not resist. He took her hands, her fingers cold in his. "What is it, Shan?"

"I… I'm supposed to be a doctor, Jack. It's what I was made for. At first, I think I considered it as a way to make my father love me, to prove I was worthy, but now I feel like it's something bigger than that. I'm meant for it."

"I know. Sometimes I wished you weren't, that you would be happy being a rancher's wife, but that was selfish. You were meant to be a doctor, born to it."

She nodded. "This whole experience, though, it's made me realize that I wasn't made to do it alone."

He stared. "Yeah?"

"Yeah." She turned tender eyes on him. "Jack, I love you."

Had she said it? Had he imagined it? He blinked hard. *Jack, I love you.*

"I've loved you since I was a teenager," she said. "I tried to stop, and it didn't work."

He couldn't answer. He knew what was coming next. The "but I can't stay married to you" speech. He shook his head and stood. "Shannon, you don't have to—"

She got to her feet and silenced him with two fingers across his lips. "Just listen."

If he could just look away from those iridescent eyes, maybe he could get out with his heart intact, but he could not. He had to stare into the face of the woman he loved desperately, foolishly, passionately, and watch her walk away from him for the last time.

She breathed out. "I want us to stay married."

He jerked. "What?"

"I want us to stay married. I need to finish my residency in Los Angeles, and then I want to find a position close to Gold Bar, close to Dina and Annabell." She breathed out long and slow. "I want to live here as your wife, Jack. And maybe someday, we can have a baby of our own."

He gaped, struck completely dumb.

She traced one hand along his cheek, igniting

sparkles that trailed through his body. Still, he was waiting for her to say he'd gotten it wrong, that she could not find happiness here with him in Gold Bar. That he'd misheard, misread, misunderstood.

"But…"

She pressed her mouth to his, and still he stood there like a stump, the warmth of her kiss bubbling through him. She was looking at him now, reaching her hand into her pocket. Easing back from him, she pulled out a ring, the wedding ring he'd given her all those years ago, when their future stretched before them like a smooth, easy trail. The one she'd recently stripped off her finger and offered to give back. "I've been a fool, and I've wasted seven years that I could have spent showing you how much I love you. I'm sorry."

"Shannon…"

"I love you, Jack Thorn." She held up the gold band sparkling with diamonds. "Will you put it on me? Will you have me as your wife for real this time?"

His legs almost would not hold him. He sank to his knees, taking the ring with him. Laying his head in her cupped hands, he breathed in the sweet silk of her skin, soaked in the gentle touch that he'd longed for since the day he met Shannon Livingston. Somewhere from the deep well inside, he found the words.

"I love you, Shan. I love you so much. Will you be my wife?"

Tears sparkled in her eyes as she looked down at him. "Yes, Jack. Yes, I will."

He slipped the ring on her finger, and for a long moment, neither of them moved. Then he stood and wrapped her in a hug so big, it gathered up all the years of pain and struggle. He kissed his wife with enough conviction to send the message loud as springtime thunder.

Forevermore, in sickness and health, for better or worse, every moment of every day, Shannon was his wife.

* * * * *

Look for the other
GOLD COUNTRY COWBOYS
stories available now:

COWBOY CHRISTMAS GUARDIAN
TREACHEROUS TRAILS

Dear Reader,

Oh, boy! My heart did a little two-step as this cowboy series galloped into the third book. It touched on themes near and dear to my heart: family, loyalty, faith, love and the power of God to sweep away our deepest misconceptions in a brief moment. It seems to me, dear reader, that in all of our efforts and striving, we are searching for perfect love, a way to ease that empty space inside that only God can fill. Shannon believes she can find what she craves through work, in the face of her earthly father's rejection. It will take many factors to help her see the truth: Jack, her mother, a relentless gang and the perfect innocence of a newborn baby. So come along on this journey with me through Gold Country. I hope the story will touch your heart the way it has mine! As always, I love to hear from my readers. You can find me on all the usual cyberstops: Facebook, Instagram, Twitter and Pinterest, as well as my website, danamentink.com, where you can find a physical address, as well. Thank you for riding along with me, dear reader. God bless you!

Sincerely,
Dana Mentink

Get 4 FREE REWARDS!

We'll send you 2 FREE Books plus 2 FREE Mystery Gifts.

Love Inspired® books feature contemporary inspirational romances with Christian characters facing the challenges of life and love.

FREE Value Over **$20**

Get 4 FREE REWARDS!

We'll send you 2 FREE Books <u>plus</u> 2 FREE Mystery Gifts.

Harlequin® Heartwarming™ Larger-Print books feature traditional values of home, family, community and most of all—love.

FREE Value Over **$20**

YES! Please send me 2 FREE Harlequin® Heartwarming™ Larger-Print novels and my 2 FREE mystery gifts (gifts worth about $10 retail). After receiving them, if I don't wish to receive any more books, I can return the shipping statement marked "cancel." If I don't cancel, I will receive 4 brand-new larger-print novels every month and be billed just $5.49 per book in the U.S. or $6.24 per book in Canada. That's a savings of at least 19% off the cover price. It's quite a bargain! Shipping and handling is just 50¢ per book in the U.S. and 75¢ per book in Canada*. I understand that accepting the 2 free books and gifts places me under no obligation to buy anything. I can always return a shipment and cancel at any time. The free books and gifts are mine to keep no matter what I decide.

161/361 IDN GMY3

Name (please print)

Address   Apt. #

City   State/Province   Zip/Postal Code

Mail to the **Reader Service:**
IN U.S.A.: P.O. Box 1341, Buffalo, NY 14240-8531
IN CANADA: P.O. Box 603, Fort Erie, Ontario L2A 5X3

Want to try two free books from another series? Call 1-800-873-8635 or visit www.ReaderService.com

*Terms and prices subject to change without notice. Prices do not include applicable taxes. Sales tax applicable in N.Y. Canadian residents will be charged applicable taxes. Offer not valid in Quebec. This offer is limited to one order per household. Books received may not be as shown. Not valid for current subscribers to Harlequin Heartwarming Larger-Print books. All orders subject to approval. Credit or debit balances in a customer's account(s) may be offset by any other outstanding balance owed by or to the customer. Please allow 4 to 6 weeks for delivery. Offer available while quantities last.

Your Privacy—The Reader Service is committed to protecting your privacy. Our Privacy Policy is available online at www.ReaderService.com or upon request from the Reader Service. We make a portion of our mailing list available to reputable third parties that offer products we believe may interest you. If you prefer that we not exchange your name with third parties, or if you wish to clarify or modify your communication preferences, please visit us at www.ReaderService.com/consumerschoice or write to us at Reader Service Preference Service, P.O. Box 9062, Buffalo, NY 14240-9062. Include your complete name and address.

HW18

HOME on the RANCH

YES! Please send me the **Home on the Ranch Collection** in Larger Print. This collection begins with 3 FREE books and 2 FREE gifts in the first shipment. Along with my 3 free books, I'll also get the next 4 books from the Home on the Ranch Collection, in LARGER PRINT, which I may either return and owe nothing, or keep for the low price of $5.24 U.S./ $5.89 CDN each plus $2.99 for shipping and handling per shipment*. If I decide to continue, about once a month for 8 months I will get 6 or 7 more books, but will only need to pay for 4. That means 2 or 3 books in every shipment will be FREE! If I decide to keep the entire collection, I'll have paid for only 32 books because 19 books are FREE! I understand that accepting the 3 free books and gifts places me under no obligation to buy anything. I can always return a shipment and cancel at any time. My free books and gifts are mine to keep no matter what I decide.

268 HCN 3760 468 HCN 3760

Name	(PLEASE PRINT)	
Address		Apt. #
City	State/Prov.	Zip/Postal Code

Signature (if under 18, a parent or guardian must sign)

Mail to the **Reader Service:**

IN U.S.A.: P.O. Box 1867, Buffalo, NY. 14240-1867
IN CANADA: P.O. Box 609, Fort Erie, Ontario L2A 5X3

* Terms and prices subject to change without notice. Prices do not include applicable taxes. Sales tax applicable in NY. Canadian residents will be charged applicable taxes. This offer is limited to one order per household. All orders subject to approval. Credit or debit balances in a customer's account(s) may be offset by any other outstanding balance owed by or to the customer. Please allow 3 to 4 weeks for delivery. Offer available while quantities last. Offer not available to Quebec residents.

READERSERVICE.COM

Manage your account online!

- Review your order history
- Manage your payments
- Update your address

We've designed the
Reader Service website
just for you.

Enjoy all the features!

- Discover new series available to you,
  and read excerpts from any series.
- Respond to mailings and special
  monthly offers.
- Browse the Bonus Bucks catalog and
  online-only exculsives.
- Share your feedback.

Visit us at:
ReaderService.com